DARKNESS ENDURED

Julia C. Hoffman

Cover Design by Chrissy Long
Cover Photo by Rachael E. Barbash
Photo of author by John Walcott, Walcott Studios Columbus, WI

ISBN-10: 0-9963974-2-6
ISBN-13: 978-0-9963974-2-1

To my daughters—Anne and Kate, it has been my pleasure to see the world through your new eyes.

Acknowledgements

Many thanks to my early readers: Mary Probst, Mary Lou Sharpee, Jackie Burke, Fran Zimmerman, and Lieutenant Alecia Rauch.

Additional thanks:

To Lieutenant Alecia Rauch for assistance in police procedure.

To my editor, Lourdes Venard, for her excellent help in showing me the errors of my way.

To Chrissy Long for another excellent cover design.

To Rachael Barbash for a wonderful cover photo.

As always, I'd like to blame someone for the errors in this book, but I am the culprit and cannot escape blame.

ONE

THE SHAFT OF sunlight caught Edie Swift by surprise. She stood in its center. Her flannel-lined bathrobe slid from her shoulders to lay crumpled on the floor around her feet as she soaked in the sun's rays. She stood until its warmth penetrated her bones.

She opened her winter-weary eyes and saw across the road a ragged patch of green creeping out from farmer Breitenbach's shed, touching the retreating snow. Spring had come. She rushed to open all the windows in her house; there was no longer a need to protect against the Arctic blasts. Now it was time to invite in the spring zephyrs to push out the closeted air of winter. The breezes did not disappoint; a warm southern wind, tempered by the snowfields it crossed, swirled through her house. And the chattering of the birds was carried with it. It smelled wonderful. It felt delicious as it caressed her skin, which was finally unwrapped from its winter layers of clothes. It sounded exciting.

Edie changed into her running gear, bundled her daughter, Hillary, into a snowsuit, and then buckled her into the jogging stroller. The county road that ran in front of her house, now free of snow and ice, beckoned. It was an April morning. Spring. And glorious. Edie needed to be part of it.

At the edge of her driveway, Edie hesitated as she decided which way to go . . . or so she told herself. Was it to be north into open farm country, or south into the village? She was sick of Troutbeck. On winter days, when she felt able to negotiate the snow and ice-clogged roads, Hillary's caregivers, pushing a bundled Hillary in the jogging stroller, insisted that they walk into the village. And, because they were older women, and moved slower than she, Edie acquiesced. Today there was no hand on her shoulder or cough to announce the woman's presence and offer restraint. It took Edie a moment to realize that today was hers to command.

Edie took a deep breath, pushed the stroller into the road and turned north, away from the village. Edie was tired of the confines of Troutbeck. Going north felt like freedom to her. Freedom from heavy winter clothes. Freedom from the confines of her house. Freedom from someone looking over her shoulder. Freedom from someone insisting they tag along. Freedom that she had craved each winter day. Freedom to make decisions that didn't impact anyone. Today belonged to her and Hillary for exploring the world.

Along the way, Edie pointed out to her daughter the tiny marvels of the country, the snow clinging to the corn stubble in the farmer's fields next door, and, in the north-facing ditches, the many layers of snow deposited by wind and snowplows that steadfastly refused to melt under the sun's intense rays. They watched as two robins dug for worms and as a pair of tall, gray birds with red-capped heads picked their way through the farm fields searching for food. But most of all, Edie found joy in stretching out her legs and testing herself against the memories of what she had once been able to do.

Edie was almost to the county line, her goal for this run, when she heard the first siren. She stopped. Listened.

Then counted three more sirens. She listened for a moment longer; the sirens sounded as if they were converging on Troutbeck. Instinct overcame the freedom of the road. Edie turned the jogging stroller around and headed back into the village. "Well, little one," she said to Hillary, "guess we're not ready for the Crazy Legs run this year. Do you remember last year when you and I ran it? Of course you don't, you hadn't made your world appearance yet. We didn't make good time during that run, but we finished. We finished. I don't want to miss this year's run. But it looks like I started training too late. I'll have to figure out something else. Maybe you and I can walk it? Does that sound like a plan to you?" Edie slowed to a walk in order to catch her breath. With a second wind, she pushed herself to a faster pace. Between running and walking, she and Hillary made it back to Troutbeck in a pathetic twenty minutes. She had miles to go, she told herself, before she regained what had been lost during her long recovery.

By the time Edie and Hillary arrived at the Troutbeck church, bunches of people stood crowding the cordoned-off area. The crime scene tape stretched across the front of the church and the roads on either side of it, which led back to the cemetery. A sheriff's car was parked in front of the tape at each driveway entrance to ensure that no one went in. A deputy sheriff leaned against each car, assessing the crowd of gawkers. Edie thought the redundancy of caution really wasn't needed in Troutbeck. Which of these old people lining the tape was going to cross the barrier for a closer look? Granted, Edie thought, most of them were baby boomers, and you could never tell what that generation would do. Some got whacked in the head in Chicago '68, others voted into office some politicians who rivaled the Know Nothings of the 1850s, and they flouted traditions and authority.

That bunch was completely unpredictable—you had to be careful, even when they turned into old people. On second thought, Edie decided it was better to keep the police tape up—just in case. You never could tell about those baby boomers.

Edie spotted Phil Best, her partner, in the crowd. He wore a winter jacket with the collar turned up against the cool breeze. His hands pushed deep into his jacket's pockets. He faced north away from the action in the cemetery, as if he were waiting for somebody. Edie pushed Hillary over to him. As she got closer, she could see Phil's lips pressed tightly together and the sadness in his eyes. Phil bent down and tucked Hillary's straying blanket around her. He took off his coat, slipped it around Edie, and then zipped her into it.

"Why do that? And why are you wearing a winter jacket? It's a beautiful spring day," Edie asked.

"It is a beautiful April morning. Almost makes you believe spring is here. But April can fool you," Phil replied.

"Spring is here. On our jog out of town, we saw these tall gray birds—"

"Sandhill cranes."

"And robins."

"Were they the resident robins, or the migrating ones?"

"There's a difference?'

"Yes. Tell me when you see red-winged blackbirds, and then I'll believe spring is here."

"But there are tulips—"

"Those bulbs are usually planted near houses. A house's concrete foundation absorbs the sun's rays then radiates it back out and, combined with heat loss from the building, it's the first place the ground might thaw and the bulbs can make their appearance in this climate."

"That's quite a technical analysis, which I already know. But why won't you believe that it's spring?"

"Because it's April. It's springlike today, but who knows what tomorrow will bring?" He leaned across the stroller to give Edie a kiss and whispered, "Remember, you are still on leave. What's going on in the cemetery isn't any of your business." Phil walked past Edie, shoved his hands into his jean pockets, and with hunched shoulders and his head down, he trudged back toward his shop.

"I haven't resigned from the force. And in case you forgot, I'm back on active duty come Monday," Edie whispered, as she watched him walk away.

Somebody, nudging past her, brought Edie's attention back to the churchyard. "Oh, it's you," she said, recognizing the historian. "What are you doing here?'

"Same as everyone else, I want to know what's going on. Also, I'm taking notes on who's here. We don't often get police action like this during the day."

"What are you going to do with the notes?"

"They go into the Troutbeck annals. Depending on what your people find here, I may interview some of these people later." The historian scanned the crowd. "Maybe you can help me. I know everyone here, except that man at the tape."

Edie, more than a little pleased to have the Dane County deputies identified as "her people," looked where the historian was pointing. "That's Mark Uselman, a reporter."

The historian wrote down his name, and then resumed meandering through the crowd, taking notes.

Edie made her way to Mark Uselman. "So, what do you know about all these deputies being here?"

"Body in the cemetery," Mark said, keeping his eyes glued to the action in the cemetery.

"What's unusual about that?" Edie continued.

"This one's dead."

"Aren't they all?"

Uselman turned to Edie with an exasperated look on his face at the questioning. "It's you. Didn't expect you here. I've gotten used to you not being at these crime scenes. Thought you were on leave?"

"I am."

"Then what are you doing here?"

Edie thought her running clothes and her pushing a baby in a stroller were dead giveaways. Apparently not. "And you call yourself an investigative reporter. Maybe you should find another profession."

Mark's face turned red as he took in her jogging suit and the baby. "Your backyard?"

"Yeah. What have you found out?"

"Not much. Call came into 9-1-1. Dead body found in the Troutbeck cemetery, gunshot. I pulled in behind a number of squads. No one's told us anything, yet. What do you know?"

"Nothing."

"Come on, Edie, you know nothing?"

"I'm out of the loop on this one, still on leave until Monday."

"But you live in this speed trap, you gotta know something."

"I don't know now, but I will . . . soon."

Both Edie and Mark turned back to watch the scene among the tombstones. Edie had been at plenty of these crime scenes. Those were her people pouring over the crime scene, and she belonged among them, not on the public's side of a police tape. She was able to identify each person working the cemetery and knew what their job for the day was. The medical examiner, Sadie Carpenter, Ben Harris, and other crime scene investigators were there, as was Luke Fitzgerald and other deputies, detectives, and the unmistakable profile of Lieutenant Gracie Davis. Yes, soon she would know what was back there. Her buddies in brown would tell, she was confident of that. She and Mark watched as the bagged body was lifted onto a gurney and put into the ME vehicle. An old man was helped to his feet and escorted down the long drive by two deputies.

"Who's the old man?" Mark whispered.

"He looks like Harold Acker. Is that Deputies Smith and Johnson escorting him?"

"More like carrying him, yes. Those two seem to be inseparable, which is good, as I think they share one brain."

As the trio advanced, Edie could see Smith and Johnson scan the crowd, which was pushing against the flimsy crime scene tape. Then the deputies brought their attention back to the dried-up old man, who looked as if the light southerly breeze would blow him away, and who seemed to trip over every pebble on the road.

"Is he a suspect? Where are you taking him?" Mark shouted to the deputies as they got closer.

"Home," said Johnson.

"Morning, Edie," said Smith. "Know this man?"

"Harold Acker, he lives a few blocks down the road," Edie replied.

"Anyone at his house?" asked Smith.

"I don't know. I think he lives alone. And it looks like most everyone in Troutbeck is here."

"He lives alone," a voice from somewhere behind Edie confirmed. "I'll go home with him." Sera Voss stepped out of the crowd, ducked under the tape, then stood by Harold. She gave him a smile and a pat on his hand that held the cane. At the squad car, Sera and Smith assisted Harold into the backseat of the squad, and then Sera slid in beside him. Harold moved closer to Sera, who slipped her arm through his.

Edie turned back to watch the scene on the hill. She'd been at a lot of scenes like this, first as a deputy, then as detective, and throughout the years had performed each task: every inch of the scene was photographed, deputies on hands and knees were scouring the area for evidence, a few were taking measurements. All this evidence would be put together and handed to the DA's office when someone was identified as the suspect. Every atom of her body was screaming to be out there in the cemetery. But she would have to wait until Monday to get the full story, unless her brothers and sisters in uniform held true to their bonds and told her something.

Edie, and a few gawkers, stayed until the deputies on the hill began to wrap up; most were packing up their gear, while a few deputies walked the crime scene again. The TV reporters took this for their cue for a press conference and drifted toward an area that they thought was the best backdrop for a photo op during their interview with Lieutenant Davis. Uselman joined them. Edie did not. She knew how the day unfolded, that only basic information would be released tonight, and that stuff she could learn on the evening news. What she wanted were the details. Edie went her own way, to the driveways that each squad would have to pass.

Edie chose the western driveway's exit to stand; it might put most of the church between her and Gracie. Maybe the deputies, her brothers and sisters in blue, but in this case brown, would tell her something before they left, if they could be sure that they were out of Gracie Davis's line of vision.

Edie knew her coworkers. They saw her and they couldn't keep their mouths shut. But what they said was quick and dirty, no more than a one- or two-word description of what they knew about the crime. They were conscious of Gracie Davis's presence—no one wanted to be seen chatting with Edie; they wanted to save their butts.

With the information that the deputies dropped for her ears only, Edie pieced together that the victim was male, thirty years old, killed from a gunshot taken at a distance, a Nicholas Klein. The exact location of the shooter hadn't been pinpointed; they'd figure that out when the reconstructionist was finished. In return, they wanted to know if the victim's name meant anything to Edie. No, she told them, as she kept an eye out for Gracie.

Sadie Carpenter, on her way to her car, stopped by Edie and spent the longest time with her. "I haven't released the scene. You are not on duty. The police tape is up to keep people like you out. Don't go in," Sadie said, then turned away, walked to her car, got in, and then drove away.

Nice seeing you too, thought Edie as she walked toward the press conference area where Gracie Davis was holding center stage.

"Lieutenant, what can you tell us about the victim?" Leigh Stone started the grilling of the lieutenant.

"Male, gunshot, more details will be released after the medical examiner has completed an autopsy, and any personal information about the victim will be released when his relatives are notified."

Leigh Stone pressed for more information. "Can you give us more details? What type of gun was used? Was the victim a local resident? Do the residents of this village need to be concerned about more violence?"

"No, I think this is an isolated incident and that the residents of Troutbeck do not need to take extraordinary precautions," said Lieutenant Davis.

"Is the victim young? Old? A vagrant?" Morris Brennan asked.

"As you know, we will release more information when the family has been notified. I don't think this community has anything to worry about," said Lieutenant Davis. She stood her ground and watched as the TV crews left her to hunt for a pliable local resident who wanted to be interviewed for local color about the crime. Left alone, Gracie Davis walked to her car. Gracie avoided eye contact with Edie as she passed her and Hillary. But Edie didn't want to be ignored. When she finally caught up with Gracie, she kept pace with Gracie's long stride and tried to start a conversation, "Good morning, Lieutenant."

There was no response.

At her squad, Gracie spoke, "Morning, Edie, and you too, Hillary. Remember, you are on leave until Monday."

"Yes, I've heard. Everyone's been reminding me. What can you tell me about the body?"

"It's dead and this is Luke Fitzgerald's case."

"When did Luke make detective?"

"A few months ago. See you Monday, and get that baby inside," Gracie said as she got into her car and drove away.

"I'm still on the force, but with an attitude like yours, I should resign. And my baby is fine where she is, thank you very much," Edie said softly to herself.

TWO

IT WAS A long-standing custom, known to everyone in Troutbeck, that the local men gathered at the Troutbeck Bar and Gas to exchange information, but the women sat around in Carole Rhyme's hair salon to gossip. Edie decided to join the women.

Edie, with Hillary asleep in her arms, walked into Carole's salon. The room went silent as she entered. Everyone, except Carole, who was busy with a customer, eyed the newcomers.

Carole rinsed Lisa VandenHuevel's hair, and then looked up. "Hi, Edie, you look cold. Grab a blanket and some coffee; you're making the rest of us cold just looking at you in that outfit."

"But it's spring," said Edie.

"Only by the calendar," said a well-groomed, dark haired woman.

"And around here, it isn't spring. It's known as mud season," said Lisa.

"Yeah, that's right," said Carole. "Out here there's winter, mud season, summer, fall. I've heard it's different for you city folks."

"What's wrong with us city folk?" Edie demanded.

"I've been asking that question myself for years," said a young woman who was sitting in the corner.

"Nothing that some time in the country wouldn't fix," said Carole.

"Carole, didn't you start out as a city girl?" Edie asked.

"Yes she did, just like most of us here," said Lisa.

"If you can call a town with a population of less than two thousand a city," said the dark haired woman.

"In Wisconsin, you can. Just yanking your chain a bit, Edie. Do you know these women?" Carole asked. "Everyone, this is Edie Swift and her daughter, Hillary. She and Phil live in Gladys Heyden's old house, next to Sera."

"We know where she lives. We've seen her walking around the village, just never had a chance to meet her," said the dark-haired woman.

Edie wondered what she was doing in Carole's salon; she didn't need any of Carole's professional help.

"Hi, I'm Bridget Briggs. I'm the high school principal. My family and I live in the Halloween House. I'm here because there's no school today."

That was it, Edie thought, *she's keeping up appearances.*

"You don't have to account for every minute of your time, Bridget," said Carole.

"Yes, I do. Ever listen to the old men at the gas station rant about school spending, and how easy our jobs are? According to them, I signed my life away when I took this principal position. I'm stopping the wild rumors before they get started. Learned that early in my career," said Bridget. "Edie, looks like you and I will be competing for Matilda's babysitting services."

"We don't refer to your house as the Halloween House," said Lisa.

"Why not? The kids do. Some of them call it the witch's house and probably worse. One of these years I hope to persuade my husband not to put up that stupid witch," replied Bridget.

"Respect, Bridget, we have respect for you," said Lisa, walking back to Carole's cutting station. "I'm Lisa VandenHuevel, the babysitter's mother. We live on the other side of Sera. Sorry I haven't stopped by earlier. You know how one thing leads to another and pretty soon your good intentions fly out the window. And when you have kids, there never seems to be enough time to do anything but their stuff."

"I'm Mariah Collins, I live outside of town. Here take my seat, your baby must be getting heavy to hold," said the young woman, standing up. Edie guessed her to be not much younger than herself.

"Nice meeting you all. I'm guessing that you've read about me, or heard about me from Carole," Edie said, as she sat down in Mariah's chair, then unzipped Hillary's snowsuit.

"There are no secrets in Troutbeck," said Lisa.

"What a beautiful baby, may I hold her?" Mariah asked.

Edie was doubtful. "She's a light sleeper."

"Oh, give her the baby and get yourself some coffee . . . and that blanket to wrap yourself up in," said Carole.

Edie settled Hillary into Mariah's arms. Mariah started swaying from side to side. Hillary softly sighed, but continued to sleep.

"Seems like you have a way with babies," said Edie.

"Never have before," whispered Mariah, smiling at Hillary.

Edie unzipped Phil's jacket and poured herself a cup of coffee before sitting down again.

"Lots of commotion over in the cemetery, know anything about it?" Carole asked the question everyone in the room was dying to ask.

"Body found," said Edie.

"An old one or a new one?" asked Carole.

"A fresh one."

"It seems as if half the cops in the county were there, so I assume it wasn't a natural death?" Lisa asked.

"I'm not assuming anything," Edie replied.

"Have they released a name?" Bridget asked.

"No, a name is released only after the next of kin has been notified, standard procedure," said Edie. Her months of medical leave spent in Troutbeck hadn't loosened her tongue.

The salon door opened. The chatter stopped. Everyone turned to see who would step in.

Carole looked up from cutting Lisa's hair. "Hi, Crystal, what are you doing here? I don't have you down for an appointment until next week."

"Meeting up with Mariah. We have a lunch date and then we'll do some shopping afterward."

Carole introduced Edie and Crystal Mitchell.

"I've heard about you," said Crystal.

"Hope it's all been good," said Edie.

"What took you so long?" Mariah asked. "Carole finished with me half an hour ago."

"Sorry, Lee wanted to drop me off here before he left for the weekend. But he didn't finish packing for his hunting trip until a few minutes ago," Crystal replied.

"What's he shooting this weekend?" Lisa asked.

"Turkey. He and one of his hunting buddies have permits for this week."

"Has he ever got one?" Bridget asked.

"None that I've ever had to clean, thank God," said Crystal. "Ready, Mariah?"

"Yes," said Mariah, as she handed the sleeping Hillary back to Edie. "She's such a sweet baby, thanks for letting me hold her."

The door opened. The talk stopped.

"Busy place," Edie observed.

Carole stopped cutting Lisa's hair. "Don't I wish." Two deputies walked in. "What can I do for you, officers?"

"Nothing ma'am, we've found the person we wanted," said Deputy Smith. "Hi, Edie."

"Everyone, this is Deputy Smith and Deputy Johnson. How'd you know where to find me?" Edie asked.

"The lady who helped us with Mr. Acker thought you might be here," said Smith.

"I've lived in Troutbeck less than seven months and everyone knows my routine," said Edie.

"Routine, it's a part of motherhood," said Lisa.

"Nothing else to do in these parts," said Bridget.

"What can I do for you two?" Edie asked, returning her attention to Smith and Johnson.

"Wanted to update you on the Washington case," said Johnson.

The quiet roomer got quieter.

Edie let out a deep sigh. "Can't it wait until Monday, when I'm back in the office?"

"Since we're here, thought we'd take the opportunity," said Johnson. "Found the jeep that was reported stolen that night."

"Where?" Since she couldn't shut the two up, she could at least keep it from getting out of hand.

"Baraboo bluffs," said Smith.

"On one of the backroads. Homeowners found it when they came to open their cottage for the summer," said Johnson.

"The ME hasn't made a positive ID of the body," said Smith.

15

"Not much left of that body," said Johnson. "May take a while for that ID."

Edie didn't need any more information on that case, and neither did anyone else in the salon, she thought. Edie tried to redirect the flow of information. "Saw Luke Fitzgerald at the crime scene, when did he make detective?"

"A few months ago," said Smith. He didn't take the hint to shut up. "Guess who the jeep is registered to?"

"LeRoy Theis, Eric's father," Smith and Johnson said in unison.

"One more thing for the DA to add to his case," said Edie.

"Yeah, wish they could move that case along," said Johnson.

"You know how it is when you get lawyers involved, just part of the system," said Smith. He pulled a notebook from his shirt pocket, and then flipped through it. "Edie, maybe you can help us. Do you know where the Nicholas Klein place is?"

Mariah Collin's face went white. Edie pushed Hillary into Johnson's arms, grabbed a wastebasket, and shoved it toward Mariah. Bridget grabbed a towel and soaked it down with cold water. Carole dropped her scissors, stepped next to Mariah, then pushed her down to the floor beside the wastebasket and, as Mariah began to puke, held her hair back.

"Look what you did!" Johnson shouted at Smith.

Hillary woke and began to cry.

"What, I didn't say anything!" Smith yelled back. "Look what you did to that baby."

"Boys, shut up," Edie ordered, as she took her crying baby from Johnson.

When Mariah finished puking, Bridget and Carole eased her to the floor. Lisa placed a couple of clean towels under Mariah's head, and Bridget placed the wet towel across Mariah's forehead.

Edie turned to give Crystal, the only one not assisting Mariah, her baby. Crystal was turning white. Edie kept the baby. "Crystal, sit on the floor. NOW," she commanded.

Crystal sat, and then she, too, lay on the floor.

"Carole, can you take Hillary?"

"Sorry, got my hands full. Try Bridget," said Carole, emptying the wastebasket of Mariah's vomit.

Edie handed Hillary to Bridget, and then turned on the deputies. "Boys, I want to see you outside."

Smith and Johnson followed Edie, who led them away from the house to the driveway, well out of the hearing range of everyone in the salon.

A cool northwest wind had replaced the southern breeze. For Edie, it was a relief from the overheated salon. "Boys, keep your voices down. Now, what do you want to tell me?"

Johnson ignored Edie and laid into Smith. "You stupid ass."

"What? It was a simple request. I didn't say anything about him being dead," Smith said.

He was interrupted by Carole when she stepped out of the salon and placed the wastebasket near the door, "Excuse me, Edie; Mariah is Nicholas Klein's wife." She frowned at Smith and Johnson, and then went back inside, letting the door slam behind her.

"You two know better than that," Edie began.

"Why are you yelling at us? I didn't say anything about why we wanted to see him," protested Smith.

"Keep your voices low. These people aren't dumb. They can put two and two together," said Edie.

"What does that mean?" asked Johnson.

Edie saw she would have to spell it out for the men. "Meaning that our deputies were out in force in this village today. A dead man was found in the village cemetery, possibly murdered. And now two of those cops are asking where a resident of this village lives. They've done the math."

"Still don't add up to him being the dead man," said Smith.

"Enough. You two zip your mouths. I'll do the talking. Follow me." Edie returned to the salon.

Smith and Johnson went through the motion of zipping their mouths before following her in. Mariah and Crystal were sitting in chairs sipping water. Bridget was holding Hillary and walking the floor in an attempt to quiet her. Carole was blow-drying Lisa's hair. All conversation stopped when Edie and the deputies entered the room.

"Officers, Nick Klein is my husband. What do you want with him?" Mariah said in a voice barely audible.

"These officers didn't tell me," said Edie. "They only said they needed to talk with him. Is he at home?"

"He should be at work," Mariah replied. "Can it wait until he gets home?"

"I think these officers would like to talk with him now."

"Don't know if he can take time from work. I could call him and ask when's the best time for them to drop by."

"Why don't you go home to do that? You'll have more privacy, if you call him from there," Edie suggested.

"But Crystal and I are going shopping," Mariah protested.

"Shouldn't take long, ma'am," said Johnson.

"Okay with you, Crystal?" Mariah asked.

"Sure. We can make lunch at your place, and then go into Madison for shopping," said Crystal.

"Mariah, Crystal, are you two feeling well enough to drive?" Edie asked.

Both women nodded, and then each took another sip of water before handing their glasses back to Carole. Mariah put on her jacket while Crystal waited by the door.

"Better zip up, it's getting chilly out there," Edie advised the women. Mariah and Crystal obediently zipped their jackets. Edie walked over to Johnson and Smith. "Don't screw up," she whispered.

Edie watched as Johnson and Smith followed Mariah and Crystal out of Carole's drive. For a moment she considered following them, but her daughter was in the room. Edie turned back to get her.

"Well?" said Carole.

"Well, what?" Edie took Hillary from Bridget and walked up and down the room, trying to quiet her.

"Edie, do I have to spell it out?" Carole asked.

"Yes, Carole, you do."

Carole took a deep breath, then let it out slowly through pursed lips. "Edie, is Nick Klein the dead man found in the Troutbeck cemetery?"

Edie hesitated. She knew these women had put two and two together when Smith let his mouth work overtime, even if Mariah and Crystal hadn't done the math. "You ladies didn't hear it from me."

The joy of spring seemed to be sucked out of the room.

THREE

THE WIND HAD changed directions while Edie was at Carole's salon. It now came more from the north, funneled directly into Troutbeck via the north-south county highway—the village's own polar express. By the time Edie got home, she was shivering from the cold. She had ignored the dropping temperature and wind changes to find more information about the body in the cemetery.

Edie took Hillary out of her snowsuit and placed her in the Pack'N Play in the family room before building a fire in the woodstove. Carole was right—she wasn't dressed for the weather; she'd wanted spring so badly that she ignored the realities. Edie changed into wool long johns, and wrapped herself in her winter bathrobe, then retreated to her rocking chair, which she pulled closer to the spreading warmth of her woodstove.

Edie's rocker was kept next to the woodstove with Hillary's Pack'N Play nearby, well away from the stove. That stove and rocker had been a major lifeline during her recuperation. But even moving the rocker closer to the stove didn't help much today. She could feel the coming storm in her bones. After last fall, she was now a faster, and more reliable, predictor of the weather than Doppler radar. With each blast of the north wind, Edie moved her rocking chair closer to the stove.

She put her feet on the woodstove's hearth and watched as the north wind pushed spring aside. The sky became a paler blue and the clouds bunched together, creating a darkened mass. Though Edie could feel the storm coming, she couldn't decide yet if it was a winter blast that would bring snow or a cold spring rain that could bring ice, which would deepen the mud season. As she thawed and rocked, she replayed the day's events. She finally acknowledged the internal conflict that, until today, she hadn't admitted was there—whether or not to return to work.

On one hand, she told herself, there was Hillary. During Edie's long recovery, Hillary was a source of joy and amazement. Her accumulated sick leave, with some days from the bank that had been donated by her and the other deputies, let her concentrate on her daughter instead of the need to make a living. Money worries never haunted her dream these days, only the brutal, shadowy memories of last fall.

On the other hand, there was the job she had sought, trained for, and was good at—and loved. It wasn't until the dead body in the Troutbeck cemetery took the abstract of returning to work and made it concrete that she acknowledged her desire to get back to that world. The old debate about returning to work had come to a head today. It didn't take Edie long to settle the question. Hillary and work could coexist; Edie would have to find the way.

Her internal debate shifted its focus. It was clear that her coworkers didn't want her on the job, at least until Monday, except for that Sadie Carpenter, who probably liked the current status quo—Edie at home. None of the deputies had given a good detailed report about their findings in the cemetery, but each had fed her a fact or two about the crime that had been committed in her town. Nick Klein was killed by a bullet fired long distance was the sum of their reports. Not much to go on. She needed more information. But this was Luke Fitzgerald's case, her internal debate began—but it was quickly countered with *it happened in my backyard.* Sadie Carpenter was lead CSI, she probably missed something. The crime scene hadn't been released; Sadie'd be back tomorrow to finish any loose ends. But Edie's bones were telling her that there would be a storm tonight. And with that a plan developed.

Edie needed to see the crime scene before the storm hit, before it was covered in snow, or washed away by rain. The best time would be tonight, when all of Troutbeck should be asleep. But she had been told by multiple people in authority to stay away, she wasn't on active duty until Monday. Were they teasing or challenging her? Edie smiled. She didn't return to work until Monday, so the only person she had to answer to was herself. For Edie, that was all the permission that was needed.

Her dilemma had disappeared. And all was right with the world.

FOUR

PHIL, STILL IN his grease-stained work clothes, walked into the kitchen—the aromas swirling through the house had pulled him from the mudroom to the kitchen.

"It smells delicious in here, what did you thaw?" he asked.

"Nothing, except the veggies. I'm making pasta primavera for supper—a tribute to spring. And why are your dirty work clothes in this kitchen?" said Edie.

"Because I'm wearing them? A tribute to spring? Have you felt the wind tonight? We should be having something heartier."

"Nope, I'm tired of winter. I want spring to be here, so I'm sending it a message to come and stay. And yes, my bones are telling me that there will be a storm tonight—snow."

"You should change your profession to meteorology."

"No chance of that, people swear more at meteorologists than they do at cops."

"Good point. What else do you have cooking? Something with cinnamon?"

"Your cooking knowledge has improved."

"So what did you make?"

"Bread, half I made into a loaf, the other half into cinnamon rolls."

"Can I have one now?"

"They just came out of the oven. We'll have them for dessert tonight and breakfast tomorrow. Now, go change, and then say hi to Hillary while I get supper on the table."

Phil changed out of his work clothes into sweats, and then settled with Hillary into Edie's rocking chair by the woodstove. He entertained his daughter while Edie finished with supper. Hillary giggled at his funny faces, the raspberries he played on her cheek. She helped turn the pages of the Sandra Boynton board book that Phil pulled from the stack of books, and then, when the reading was done, she chewed on its corners. After Edie announced that supper was on the table, Phil fastened Hillary into her high chair, where she played her newly discovered favorite game of drop the bottle, or for variety, the cooled pasta, on the floor.

"Good science experiment, baby girl. You've proved again that gravity still exists," Phil said, setting the bottle back on the high chair tray again, and leaving the pasta on the floor to be picked up later. "Edie, this food is delicious," Phil said, taking a second helping of the pasta. "When do we get to eat the cinnamon rolls?"

Edie pushed the pasta around on her plate, and then looked up at Phil "Later. Why haven't you looked at me even once during supper, or talked to me?"

Phil put his food-laden fork on his plate and glanced at Edie. "Because Hillary is here."

"What does that mean?"

"Because if I looked at you, or talked to you, I'd start yelling. I don't want to yell, especially not in front of our baby. It could hurt her psyche or something like that," Phil said as he again picked Hillary's bottle off the floor.

"Why would you want to yell? And about what?"

"I'd like to never yell, but I don't know what else to do."

"Then let things be."

"I can't. You are planning something to do with that murder. And I already don't like it, and I don't even know the details. It's driving me nuts knowing that whatever I say won't make a dent in your plans. We need to talk."

"Then we will have a discussion about whatever is bothering you."

"Which will disintegrate into a shouting match. But we need to talk, or I'll explode."

Edie tried to read Phil's expression, but he wouldn't look at her. He kept his face turned to their daughter, with a smile on his face for her.

"Okay. You give Hillary a bath and put her to bed, I'll clean up the kitchen. Then we will have our yelling match."

When Hillary was in her crib, Edie and Phil went to their respective corners in the family room. Edie rocked in her chair by the stove. Phil sat in his armchair across from her. Separating them was the sizzling hot woodstove, and on a nearby TV tray table, a peace offering of cinnamon buns and the baby monitor. From the sounds coming across the monitor, Hillary was settling into sleep.

Phil broke the icy silence. He still couldn't look at Edie; instead, he kept his eyes locked on his clasped hands resting in his lap. "You're planning something."

"I'm always planning something. Are you accusing me of planning something nefarious?"

"Come on, Edie, we've lived together for a long time now. When you fix a meal like tonight's, you're planning something that you shouldn't be doing."

"Good to know you are paying attention. We could use you on the force. Ever thought of changing professions?" Edie made a mental note to prepare extraordinary meals at irregular intervals from now on.

"And I'm guessing your plans have something to do with the dead man in the cemetery."

"Yes." Why not tell the truth, Edie reasoned. It was easier to remember.

"Leave it alone, you're not on the job until Monday."

"I know, but I can't ignore a crime committed in my backyard."

"Let someone else solve it."

"That will be Luke Fitzgerald's job."

"Let him do the legwork. Consult with him later."

"But I still gotta know."

"Why?"

"Because this job that I do is part of who I am. It is what I trained for. And I'm good at it."

"I think you like the rush it gives you."

"It's better than using drugs."

"I don't like it. I don't want a repeat of last year."

At last, thought Edie, the crux of his problem—she barely survived a beating. "Neither do I."

"Quit the force. I can support the three of us. My business is doing well. My business debt is under control. You've enjoyed being with Hillary this winter. Why not stay with her a bit longer?"

"I'm not quitting."

"Damn it. I should have followed my mother's advice and married someone who'd listen to me."

"You still have time, we're not married."

"Why aren't we?"

"Because you want a little woman, and I'm not that. As for what I do for a living, that ship sailed a long time ago."

"Change it."

"I don't want to."

"You owe me."

"What do I owe you?"

"I saved your life. You owe me to not put your life in jeopardy again. And you owe that to our daughter."

"Thank you for what you did, but, as I said, that ship sailed a long time ago."

"You owe Hillary a mother who walks through that door each night after work."

"What I owe Hillary is to love her and to work for a more just world. And last time I looked, I was doing that. Do I need to point out that Hillary has two parents? That there are two of us to guide her through this world? Not just me. That we're supposed to have each other's back during this parenting stuff? And, if the unthinkable happens, each of us will step up to the plate and do what we have to."

"I can't stand this. I should never have become involved with a cop."

"Your choice, then and now."

The peace offering of cinnamon rolls was forgotten. Phil stomped off to his basement workroom. Edie moved her chair closer to the woodstove and rocked faster.

Phil clicked off the ten o'clock news and looked at Edie, who was sitting at the far end of the couch dressed in her running gear. He broke the silence that hung between them. "When are you going?"

"Soon. Troutbeck residents should be tucked into their beds and asleep by now, and the strip-club patrons of Lower Bottom won't stagger out to their cars for another three to four hours."

"Dress warm."

"Yes."

"Got your cell?"

"Wouldn't think of leaving home without it."

"Good." Phil turned away from Edie and walked toward their bedroom, then half turned back toward her with his eyes downcast. "Be careful."

"Always."

FIVE

A WINTER WIND whipped around the corner of the house and straight into Edie as she firmly pulled her front door shut. She flipped up the hood of her running jacket. Looked up and down the county highway that ran in front of her place, no vehicles—the farmers north of town were sensibly in bed. Then she looked toward Troutbeck—no lights were on, and she knew that its streets had been rolled up a long time ago. She hoped the residents were sleeping, too. It was time to execute her plan.

Her legs wouldn't move. *It's only because I'm still deciding about the run,* she tried to lie to herself. But she knew differently, she never was any good at fooling herself. It had been happening to her for a long time now. Those early times of paralysis dropped her to her knees, followed by a long crawl back to bed and a pulling of the covers over her head. It hadn't taken her long to learn the signs and the progression of the staggering fear. First, her legs wouldn't move, then her knees would tremble, then her thighs. Then fear would take hold of her guts, and she would collapse and curl into a ball until the memories she possessed of that fall night released her. If she was lucky, she wouldn't have to change her pants and underwear. It took her longer to figure out a way to deal with the overwhelming fear than to recognize it. Her knees began to shake. *Quick, a song,* she yelled silently. *Any song would do, a Rodgers & Hammerstein one, a Disney tune, a Beatles song, something from Jewel, or Smashing Pumpkins, or Bon Jovi, or that Garth Brooks song. That was it* . . . Edie softly hummed the line about friends in low places, then another line. Soon her humming morphed into whistling, and soon the whistling morphed into a tune—"Yankee Doodle Dandy." It worked. The tremors left, the jellied knees became solid again, and Edie stepped off her front step into the darkness of a country night. That was the plan all along . . . of course.

Edie jogged toward Troutbeck. At the empty corner store, she paused in its shadow to check the Troutbeck Bar and Gas. Its lights were out. Now only two lights shone in Troutbeck, both illuminating a crossroad. Edie skirted the area illuminated by the streetlight at the store, which had been placed to mark the intersection of the county highways. She took a right. Her humming turned to words, which set a cadence for her movement: she planted her left foot on "it's going to snow," her right foot on "I gotta see." She waved at the sheriff's deputy on duty in front of the church as she jogged past it, then into the darkness of the farmland between Troutbeck and Lower Bottom. There weren't any cars on the road; the drunks and patrons of the strip clubs weren't heading home yet. The night world was empty except for her. Outside of Troutbeck, no one would see her movements. Halfway to Lower Bottom, where no farm lights could expose her movements, Edie turned back to the church. The running was easier on the return to the village; the wind was at her back. It had been miserable running into the northwest wind, it was cold and damp with a bite to it. Her investigation would have to be short—snow was coming soon.

Partway back to the church came the moment of no return, the final question of should she cross the line or not. Her cadence of *it's going to snow, I gotta see* filled her thoughts and pushed aside the certainty of her dismissal or worse, if caught. But if that happened, maybe she could become a private eye, or maybe her lawyer, Brooke Rivera, needed an investigator. The *I gotta see* mantra pushed those other thoughts out of her head. She took the first step off the pavement, then another. Edie ran flat out across the farmer's field, grateful for the temperature drop that hardened the soil. She slipped under the police tape and sprinted to the church's windbreak of pines. The pines, and the clouds drifting across the moon and stars, would blur the view of any villager who stayed up late or had insomnia, and shelter her as she caught her breath and waited for her heart rate to return to normal. If anyone glanced out their window, hopefully they would mistake her for a deer. But, just in case, she kept to the pines with their low-hanging branches until she was even with the cemetery, then ran flat out to the bench where she had seen the deputies working earlier that day.

At the bench, Edie took a deep breath, reminding herself, again, that she needed to survey the death scene before the snow fell. This was where she lived. This was where she and Phil chose to raise their daughter. Her actions tonight were one more step in keeping her daughter safe. That satisfied Edie's conscience. But she still pleaded with the universe to make it snow. A moment later, she slipped a penlight from her jacket, definitely inadequate lighting for searching a crime scene at night, but the only light she was willing to risk being seen while she conducted an investigation of the area. Still, as a precaution, she cupped a hand around the tiny light to further restrict its beam. No sense in risking exposing herself more than necessary. *Damn Sadie for not releasing the crime scene.* Edie's training held, even after months away from the job. She stood in one spot until her initial survey of the scene was complete. She hoped the scene investigators had gotten all the photos they needed because she was about to add her footprints to the ones that were already there and, with her limited visibility, it seemed as if footprints were everywhere within the crime scene. Maybe hers would not be noticed by Sadie and her crew when the site was revisited.

Methodically, Edie approached the granite bench, spiraling her movements inward until she reached the bench. Even with her tiny light, she could see that the bench itself was drenched in blood. Blood, dripping from the bench, had become rivulets that coursed down the grass decline to collect in pools behind pebble dams that were now congealing. Blood seemed to be everywhere. She needed to consider each step; she didn't want her tracks to be followed. For now, Edie was more intent on the bench. That was where Nicholas Klein and death met. Edie stood silent for a moment, as she did at every death scene, an act of reverence for a life that had passed from this existence, no matter how meager it had been, and an acknowledgement of the power of death to obliterate. Edie moved to the headstone nearest the bench, Mamie Karl Acker, Beloved wife of Harold Acker; it too was splattered with blood. She looked at more headstones, all Ackers—might be a family burial plot, she thought. She followed the headstones until the Acker name ended. About twenty-five feet away, at the edge of the Acker plot, was a headstone for a Mamie Robin Neuport Brown, age 19—how sad. She wondered if the two Mamies might be related.

She squatted and did a slow sweep of the area. At the edge of her light, where the road and grass met, something glittered. Edie moved closer to the object for a better look. A fragile sliver of something shone in the light. Edie brushed away the twigs, dirt, and stones from around the clasp to find a necklace. With a twig that had been shed from a nearby maple tree Edie picked it up. Unzipping her running jacket to use as a shield, Edie examined the necklace. "How did Sadie's crew miss you?" she asked out loud. Or had someone, besides her, been in the cemetery after it was closed by the deputies? Edie looked closer at the necklace hanging from the stick. It was a daisy chain; something that might be worn by a young girl, thinning in places—someone's treasure was her assessment. Edie placed the necklace back where she found it and covered it with the dirt, gravel, and twigs that she had removed, but left more of the chain exposed. She hoped that Sadie or her crew would find it tomorrow. Edie made a mental note of its location so she could look for it when Sadie finally released the scene.

Shifting her focus, she recalled that deputies had told her the killing shot came from a distance. Edie looked for a place, other than the blood-drenched bench, that would give her a view of the land surrounding the cemetery. Where was the most likely spot the killer had dug in and waited for the prey? There was a knoll behind her to the south. Edie walked up the knoll. It was hard to believe this was the high point of the area, but from the knoll she could see for miles, even in the diminishing starlight. She was hampered in that attempt because no one had told her which way the body had fallen or the direction they assumed the shot was fired from. So she slowly whirled around and assessed the area. To the north was the solid mass of the church. To the east, at the top of a hill, sat Troutbeck, the hill covered by houses and trees. To the south was the knoll itself, only good as a cover if the shooter was behind it, which wasn't plausible. At the bottom of the knoll was a grove of trees that separated the cemetery from wetlands and farm fields. To the west stood the twin lines of pine trees, creating a windbreak, and beyond that, maybe a half-mile away, a farmstead, and beyond that a wall of snow moving toward her. She'd have to wrap up her investigation, fast. With snow moving in, she didn't have time to recreate the crime. Come Monday, she'd have to rely on everyone's report of the scene, if Gracie let them talk to her about it. She thought back to last night. Since Hillary's birth, she had become a lighter sleeper. Was there anything that made her sit up last night, or roll out of bed? No, she had not. She gave up; ice crystals were hitting her face. Enough of the speculation, it was time to go home. Edie turned off the penlight, put it back into her pocket, and zipped it shut. She sprinted to the windbreak and then retraced her cross-country run to the county highway. Edie waved to the deputy as she passed the church and then jogged the rest of the way home.

Her front door was unlocked. She'd have to talk to Phil about that. A lamp was on in the living room. She would leave it on, easier to explain a forgotten light to her watchful neighbors than one that went off in the middle of the night. The warm air of her house penetrated her jacket and running pants. She had to pee. She tried to strip off her clothes but her fingers hadn't thawed and her pants were frozen to her legs. How long had she been out? Maybe she should go outside and piss in her pants like she used to do eons ago during her long runs. But, she reasoned, the pee would freeze and cement the pants to her legs. She tried harder to wiggle out of the pants. Success. She wouldn't have to piss in her pants.

When she slipped into bed, the cold spread from Edie to Phil.

Phil reached over and pulled Edie to him, then wrapped his body around her. "You need warming."

"Got caught in the snowstorm. Were you really sleeping?"

"Yes," Phil said. He could lie too, if needed. "Have a good jog?"

Don't ask, don't tell was the policy he and Edie had agreed on at the beginning of their relationship. If Gracie ever drilled him about a case, he could truthfully say that he knew nothing. "Productive," said Edie as she fell asleep in Phil's warmth.

SIX

THE NEXT MORNING, the weather person was reporting conditions that Edie had predicted yesterday. The unexpected storm, not by Edie, had dumped eight inches of snow in the area. Cars were sliding off roads, lots of fender-benders, some head-on collisions. If you don't have to go out, stay home, was the suggestion of the day from the Dane County Sheriff, the Madison Police, and state highway patrol.

"I wonder how many people will listen to that advice. It's Saturday, how many people need to go out?" Edie asked Phil as she flipped the French toast.

"Everyone. It's a challenge. They've been told to stay home, so they need to go out. And Saturday means mall time, no matter what the weather," Phil replied.

"What is essential at the mall?" Edie asked the universe. "Seriously, people, listen to the reports of accidents. Stay home. And another thing, how can people forget how to drive in such short of time? The last winter storm was what . . . three weeks ago? They should all stay at home, and keep us safe," Edie pronounced, then flipped the golden brown French toast onto a plate and passed it to Phil, who cut it into bite-sized pieces for Hillary. He then took turns with Hillary blowing on it to cool it down. "What shall we do today?" she asked Phil.

"Take your own advice of a minute ago and stay home."

"But today's special for me, my last Saturday of leave. I want to do something. Something exciting, memorable."

"Didn't you get enough excitement last night?"

"No. It gave me the itch to do more."

That stopped their conversation. All winter she and Phil skirted the topic of her job, until last night. Yesterday's conversation was the closest they had come to talking about THE incident and her job. Edie wasn't ready and Phil didn't care to talk about it anymore.

Edie changed the subject. "Talked with Lisa VandenHuevel yesterday, you know, the one with a daughter who is of babysitting age."

"That's nice, why do we need a babysitter? We've got experienced sitters in your aunt, Sera, Carole, Gracie, my mother and sisters. Why do we need to pay a teenager?" Phil said as he picked Hillary's sippy cup off the floor.

"Our families and friends put in a lot of time babysitting this winter; they might want a break from it. Give them a chance to get back into their own lives. Besides, what if we want to go someplace and none of them are available?"

"We'll be like my parents and stay home."

"That's always your fallback solution . . . You do understand that we've got a life and they've got a life not centered on us?"

"What's wrong with the tried-and-true? And my mother couldn't live without telling me how to run my life."

Edie wasn't going to let this go. "I don't want to turn into one of those crazy old recluses."

"If we stay home, no one will know we've become crazy."

37

"I will. Once in a while, I need to get out minus the baby. I've been cooped up here all winter and yesterday reminded me of what I was missing. There is nothing to be gained by staying home all the time."

"We'd be safe and sound."

Edie stared at Phil trying to read his thoughts. It wasn't much of a challenge, they were a continuation of the short conversations they had been having since yesterday. The one skirted, the one about him and Gracie finding her clinging to life. "You knew that I was a cop when we hooked up."

"I didn't know the whole of the job."

"You and everyone else married to a cop. Or a firefighter. Or a military person. Or—"

"I didn't know it was this hard. I didn't know what it meant to sit home and worry. I'm supposed to be the protector. I'm the one who's supposed to wear the pants."

Edie walked around the island, kissed Phil, then whispered in his ear, "You get to wear them, too, unless there's a reason not to."

"Stay," Phil whispered back.

"I can't. We're asking the VandenHuevel girl to sit, sometimes." Edie sat on Phil's lap and together they watched the wintry clouds give way to blue skies, and made faces at their baby until the odor of a dirty diaper became too strong to ignore.

After breakfast, cabin fever was in full force for Edie and Phil. The road in front of their house was filled with snow. The storm had come in late, the snowplow crews were probably still clearing the primary highways. The secondary roads and those farther down the list of priorities would have to wait. The alternative, waiting for eight inches of snow to melt, might take... well ... forever was unbearable. Both were antsy after pulling the scab off the psychological wounds inflicted from last fall's incident. To keep their cabin fever at bay, and their minds occupied, they reached the last desperate resort—they cleaned their house.

By ten-thirty that morning, Edie had enough of domestic chores; the house couldn't get any cleaner. "I need to go for a run," Edie shouted to Phil as she changed into a jogging suit. After pulling on a winter-weight running top, she noticed Phil, holding Hillary, standing in their bedroom doorway.

"Could you jog to the gas station? We need some milk," Phil said, as he tucked her cell into the back pocket of her running top.

"That's not far enough for me."

"In this snow it will be, and on the return run you'll be lugging a gallon of milk through snow and slush."

"I won't be long."

"Then I'll have lunch ready when you get back. What do you want?"

"Forage for something in the freezer. We need to empty it before summer." Edie kissed Phil, then Hillary, and sprinted for the door.

SEVEN

IT WAS PLEASANT to be outside, even in snow that was the consistency of mashed potatoes that slowed her run to a walk. She moved to the road following tire tracks to the Troutbeck Bar and Gas. A few clouds in the west hung in a perfect blue sky, and snowmobiles were roaring on the trails enjoying the unexpected snow.

As the Troutbeck Bar and Gas came into view, Edie counted eight snowmobiles parked in front. *Why were they wasting time inside? This would surely be the last snow of the season. Those idiots should be out enjoying it. Or did they come just for the beer? Didn't they get enough of it last night?*

Edie's entrance into the convenience store-bar went unnoticed as the discussion at the bar changed to an argument. She stopped at the table near the entry to read the Madison paper's headline: Body Found in Local Cemetery. That headline probably got a lot of laughs before people read the story, but for sure, that paper needed a new headline writer. The background talk at the bar escalated to a shouting match; it got Edie's attention. She turned so as to see the people at the bar. All were seated, snowmobile suits hanging around their waists, with a beer and snowmobile helmet in front of them on the bar.

"I'm betting she did it," shouted a male voice.

"Doubt it, hear tell it was a long-distance shot, and I don't know of any woman that good with a gun," yelled a second.

How did the story leak out, Edie wondered, and why are these people yelling?

"Don't they always say the spouse is the first suspect?" the first man replied.

"Yeah, she probably did it. She's a bitch." A new voice added his opinion.

Edie was thinking that it was time to become part of this discussion. If she couldn't add anything, at least she'd be able to put a face to the voice. She walked to the bar and stood quietly to one side and unnoticed by the barflies as they continued their judgment of the deceased and his wife.

"What do you have against your sister-in-law, Jay?" a female voice confronted him.

"She's always sticking her nose where it don't belong. Never did let him do anything!" said Jay.

"That's not what I heard," said the first man.

"If half the gossip I heard is true, she should'a shot him a long time ago. At least had him neutered," said a second woman.

"Anyway, I doubt it was her, women usually use poison," said the second man.

"Where do you get your information from? Bob's University and Car Wash? Women use guns, too. No different than men," replied the first woman.

"And he probably deserved it," said the second woman.

A beer mug was slammed on the bar. Edie turned to see a man advancing toward one of the women. Two men rose from their stools, placing themselves between the angry man and the women.

"Cool it, Jay. Just women gossiping. They don't mean no harm," said one of the men.

"This is a tough time for you, why don't you go home and cool off," said the other man.

Mike Erdmann, the manager of Troutbeck Bar and Gas, came out of the storeroom. "I'm cutting you off, Jay. Go home. Hey, Edie, what can I do for you?" Erdmann asked. "Everyone, this is Detective Edie Swift." Silence followed his introduction, but everyone's head swiveled to look at Edie.

Jay stomped out of the bar. A few men followed him. Moments later three snowmobiles roared out of the gas station.

The remaining men and women at the bar looked at her for a moment, then turned back to finish their beers in silence. Two of the barflies pushed their half-finished beer glasses away, stood up, struggled into their snow-mobile gear, and left the building. Two of the women slid off their stools to follow.

"Look at that car," said one of the women, standing at the window. "Something's wrong with it."

"Looks like Lee Mitchell's car," said one of men who had joined her.

The patrons who were still in the bar gathered around the window to see. Lee Mitchell's car came down the hill, brake lights going on and off, and then the brake lights stayed on a bit longer. Maybe the driver miscalcu-lated the length of open road. Maybe the driver didn't see the patch of ice and snow that had built up on the road. Maybe the snow had built up in the car's wheel wells and turned to ice. Maybe the driver had forgotten how to drive in winter conditions, maybe even had a death wish to be out in such conditions, Edie thought. Whatever the reason, the car and driver veered off to the left, over the shoulder, then down into the deep ditch.

The car was stopped by the pile of snow and slush it had pushed going into the ditch.

"Call 9-1-1," Edie yelled as she pushed through the gawkers and ran out of the station. A few of the barflies followed her. Slowed by the slush, she still arrived at the car well ahead of the others. She yanked the door open. "Don't move," Edie commanded the driver, followed by, "Can you talk? Are you okay?"

The driver, not taking in Edie's commands, turned toward Edie. "I'm okay. Was that a patch of ice? Damn, I wasted my morning at work for nothing. I thought these roads would be cleared by now."

"Ma'am, can you tell me your name?" Edie asked, starting the standard the protocol to assess for alertness: person, place, and time.

"Crystal Mitchell. Could someone call my husband? Double damn, I forgot, he's hunting. Is he going to be angry about his car?"

"Crystal, I need you to not move anything. Look straight ahead. We've called 9-1-1. An ambulance will be here soon."

"You look familiar. Didn't I meet you yesterday's at Carole's?"

"Yes, you did. Now you need to stop moving."

"Why? I'm okay."

"Let the EMTs determine that. I need you to stay still and face forward."

"Damn. How am I going to get home? Lee's not there. What am I going to do?"

"We'll find someone to tow your car to your house. Listen, sounds like the ambulance is almost here and a sheriff's deputy. They'll take over."

Moments later a squad car, with an ambulance behind it, pulled into the gas station.

"Excuse me, ma'am. Thanks for your help, but I'll take over now" said the deputy walking up behind Edie. Edie backed out of the open door. "Oh, it's you, Edie. Want to work this one?"

"Can't, Johnson, I'm not on duty until Monday."

"When did that ever stop you?" Johnson replied. "Did you see the accident?"

"Yes," said Edie. With his attitude, she wasn't going to offer any more information. He'd have to pull the information out of her—*just like any other witness I've encountered.*

"Anyone else see the accident?" Johnson asked the people who had followed Edie from the station. Everyone raised their hand. "Edie, I need you to get everyone's name, address, and phone number." He pulled a notebook and pen from his pocket and held it out for Edie. She reluctantly took them.

Edie collected the information. Uncertain if Johnson would credit her with assisting him, she put her name last on the list. The small knot of people dispersed only after the ambulance left. Edie handed the notebook back to Johnson, climbed up the slippery embankment, and then started the jog home. It was at the intersection that she remembered her mission, milk. She returned to the gas station.

Edie had a hard time locating the milk section. It was pushed into a corner of the cooler to give room for the multitude of beers and pops. The whole milk's best by date was only two days away, but what was a mother to do? Edie bought it. Erdmann wasn't at the register. "Mike, I'm ready to check out," Edie yelled.

"If you got correct change, leave it on the counter," Erdmann yelled back.

"I need change."

"Be with you in a few moments."

Edie paid for the milk, but stayed at the cash register, stomping her feet to warm them up.

"Need anything else, Edie?'

"Who was that guy who stormed out of here earlier?"

"You mean Jay Klein, the dead man's brother?"

"I hadn't heard that they released the name."

"Didn't need to around here, the word spread fast. Everyone in Troutbeck knows who the dead man is."

"That brother seems like a hothead."

"Only when drunk; usually, he's an okay guy. I know his limit, even if he doesn't."

"Sounded as if he didn't think much of his sister-in-law."

"Nope, it didn't. Feel sorry for Mariah for marrying into that clan. Only a mouse of a girl would have made that lot happy."

"Why is that?"

"Their women are still supposed to be seen and not heard. They only like women in the kitchen or flat on their backs," Erdmann said and chuckled. "Not likely to make it to this century. They haven't made it to the twentieth century."

"That attitude seems to be endemic in this area," Edie said, remembering the morning's conversation with Phil. She picked up the milk and decided it would be better not to jog home and walked home in the deepening slush.

EIGHT

EDIE SAW PHIL standing at the door in his genie pose waiting for her. She had left the house with a truce between her and Phil, and returned to a warrior. Why? Then she noticed the snowmobile in the front yard. She hadn't seen this one before.

"What took you so long? Find another body?" Phil demanded.

"Accident near the station."

"And you had to work it."

"I refused to, but I witnessed it, and Johnson needed some help."

"You are not on duty."

"Responsibility of every citizen to help where we can." Edie decided no one was going to win, so she changed the subject. "Whose snowmobile?"

"Hank Erb's. He and Aunt Jill are in the kitchen with Hillary."

Edie heard laughter and her daughter's squeals of delight coming from the kitchen. "Who is this Hank Erb?"

"Local farmer. The rest of the info you need to get from Aunt Jill. By the way, your lunch is cold."

Edie dripped water from her shoes and clothes all the way to the kitchen. There, at the table, sat her Aunt Jill and Hank Erb, both in snowmobile suits unzipped to the waist. She stood in the doorway, with Phil looking over her shoulder, and watched as this Hank Erb bounced her daughter up and down and on every third bounce, did a raspberry on her cheek. Her Aunt Jill sat next to him, really almost on top of Hank Erb, thought Edie. *When did this happen?* Edie wanted to scream.

Edie watched Aunt Jill smile at Mr. Erb, kiss him on the cheek, and then notice her. Aunt Jill slid a few inches away from him. "Hi, Edie. Don't know if you've ever met Henry Erb. Hank, this is my niece, Edie Swift."

Hank stood up, still holding Hillary. He shook hands with Edie. "Nice to finally meet you. Our paths never seemed to cross, but I've heard a lot about you. Good to have you in our neck of the woods."

"Nice to meet you. Seems you have a way with children."

"Got a number of grandkids myself, but they're in other parts of Wisconsin. So I enjoy getting some grandpa time when I can, even if it is with other people's grandchildren."

Aunt Jill was staring at Edie, trying to telegraph something to her. Edie understood Aunt Jill's look. It meant that Edie should keep the conversation light and polite, and if she didn't, when they were alone it would be a different story. Edie was deciding whether or not to ignore it. For years and years, she and Aunt Jill had told each other everything. Why hadn't she been told about this Hank Erb? And who was he anyway, stealing into her aunt's life? Then Edie noticed that Aunt Jill was glowing. It was the same glow Aunt Jill had when Edie graduated from high school, and college, and got promoted to detective, and when Aunt Jill first held Hillary. Edie wondered if she had glowed like that on her first date with Phil. Edie stopped right there; she refused to let her mind wander further down that path. Edie struggled to keep her questions to acceptable subjects.

"Aunt Jill, didn't see your car. How did you get out here?" she asked.

"Hank picked me up by snowmobile earlier this morning in Madison. We didn't want to waste this last snow. You know, Hank, this storm kinda reminds me of the spring blizzard of '72."

"That was a big dump," he said. "Didn't expect it, had to shovel my way to the barn. That was the first time I swore I'd quit milking."

"When was the second?" Aunt Jill asked.

Edie noticed she was being shoved out of the conversation.

"Winter of '85-'86. The snows came and kept coming, couldn't get the rest of the crops out of the field. And that damn governor—"

"Which governor was that?" Edie asked. She decided that she should be part of the conversation. Aunt Jill was hers, and they were in her house. She would not be ignored as if she were a kid.

"Take your pick," said Hank. "They've each had their problem."

"Hank, we'd better get back to your place before we lose all the snow," said Aunt Jill.

Hank looked out the family room windows to the field next door. Black mud was visible between the rows of corn stubble. "Guess you're right. Hate to give up this little girl, though. We're having fun."

Aunt Jill took Hillary from Hank, handed her to Edie, and then kissed the two of them. "See you two Monday. Hank, we'd better get out of here, or we'll be riding through mud."

"We'll talk then," Edie said to Aunt Jill. "Nice meeting you, Hank."

Aunt Jill and Hank put on their snowmobile gear; this time it was to protect against the developing slush, not the cold of the early morning. Edie and Hillary stood at the living room picture window waving good-bye to Aunt Jill and Hank as the snowmobile eased into the field.

Phil closed the front door, and then turned to Edie. "Thought I knew everything there was to know about Edith Swift. Didn't know there was a jealous streak in her makeup."

"When were you going to tell me about Hank Erb?"

"When the time was right."

"Sooner would have been better."

"He's a local farmer. Widower. No kids in the area. Occasionally stops by the shop to shoot the breeze and ask how to fix one of his trucks."

"When did he and my aunt get together?"

"Didn't know they had hooked up." Phil sat on the couch, picked up the newspaper, and flipped to the sports section. He peeked over the top of the paper. "Is this the first time she's had a—"

"Guy? I don't know. First time she's ever introduced one to me As long as I can remember, it's always been just me and her."

"What about me? Where am I in this picture? Don't I count for something?"

"Then you came and it was the three of us."

"Then Hillary."

"And that makes four. Yes, our family expanded."

"Aunt Jill accepted that growth. Now it looks as if it's your turn to find a way to include Hank Erb," Phil said. "Think of that, I'm telling Edith Swift to put on her big-girl pants and grow up. Never thought that time would come."

Edie handed Hillary to him. "Here, she needs changing. I'll get lunch. And Crystal Mitchell needs her car towed to her place."

"Why do I have to do it?"

"The accident happened near your shop, thought you should be neighborly, so I offered your assistance."

NINE

IT WAS SUNDAY, tomorrow was back-to-work day for Edie.

At ten, Edie was still in her pajamas. So was Hillary. And it was Phil's turn to complain of having cabin fever. He was dressed and ready to go to the shop before he sat down to the breakfast Edie prepared. But after eating a stack of blueberry pancakes smothered in Wisconsin maple syrup, three strips of Nueske's bacon, juice, and coffee, he was stuffed and didn't care to move. Instead of going to the shop, he joined Edie in her favorite Sunday morning sport of yelling at the talking heads of television.

At noon, Edie and Hillary were still in their pajamas, sitting in the family room warmed by the woodstove, and watching the snow melt along the line fence. And Phil still hadn't gone to the shop.

"Isn't it time for you two to get dressed?" Phil asked.

"Why? Is there someplace we need to go? Hillary and I are enjoying watching the snow melt and the Sandhill cranes hunt for food. Besides, Hillary's nap time is soon, and I want to enjoy my last lazy Sunday at home. And in another eight hours, we'll have to put them back on. Easier to stay in them."

"That doesn't sound like you. What happened to yesterday's need to get out?"

"That was yesterday. I got over it. You are seeing the new me."

Phil started to cough.

"Are you coughing, or laughing?"

"Both."

"Meaning what?"

"Where are you hiding the real Edie Swift? The one who has only one speed—fast forward. The one who arrested me for drunk driving. The one who couldn't wait to correct the evils of the world."

"What I remember is that you pestered me for almost a year to go out with you after your arrest; thought I was going to have to get a restraining order against you. And it wasn't drunk driving; it was destruction of private property and trespassing. I couldn't arrest you for drunk driving because you and your car were standing still up against a tree. Remembering back, you barely passed a breathalyzer test. Now leave me alone, so I can enjoy the world in my pj's."

Phil picked Hillary off the floor. "I'm going to help you out. I'll put Hillary down for her nap. You get dressed."

Edie decided not to. Nobody told Edie Swift what to do, except those who signed her paycheck, but usually their demands were made as requests, or they got Gracie Davis to talk to her.

Twenty minutes later, Edie was still in her pajamas, this time thinking about work. Would it be a desk job, or would she be out on the road? If she was out on the road, would she have a partner, or go solo? What was new with the force? What had changed since she'd been gone? Could she keep up, or was she already left behind? A knock on the front door brought her back to the present.

Phil answered the door. "Hi, Sera, come on in." Edie listened from the family room. "What can we do for you?"

"I was wondering if Edie would do something for me."

"You can ask her, but she says that this is her last lazy day before work tomorrow."

"That doesn't sound like Edie. Is she sick? Maybe I should go."

"Why don't you talk with her?"

"Are you sure?"

"Yeah. Come on in. She's in the family room."

Sera poked her head into the kitchen. "Edie, can I talk with you?"

"Of course, come on back, but I'm warning you that I'm still in pj's."

"As long as you're not nude, it doesn't matter." Sera settled into Phil's chair by the woodstove across from Edie.

For a person who wanted to talk, Sera wasn't saying anything, Edie thought. Edie led the way. "Heard you tell Phil you needed help. What kind of help?"

"Are you up to helping?"

"I don't know what help you need, yet."

"I don't need the help. Harold Acker does. He wasn't in church this morning."

"The old man from the cemetery?"

Sera nodded her head.

"I wouldn't worry. He must've had quite a fright Friday and hasn't gotten over it," Edie said.

"He did take Friday's happening hard, but he always comes to church. Even after Mamie died he never missed a Sunday."

"Who is Mamie?"

"His wife, the angel in his life."

"Isn't talking to Harold the minister's job?"

"The minister wants you to talk to Harold, too."

"Why me?"

"He said you've dealt with people in situations like this before."

"I'm guessing the minister has also done that."

"I think he's scared of Harold, and says that Harold has hung up on him every time he calls him."

"Harold will probably do the same to me."

"It's my turn to take Harold some lunch; thought you could come with me, maybe talk to him at his house?"

Edie looked at Sera. She owed her so much: Sera had watched her baby girl on that night, had taken turns caring for Hillary and Edie during this long winter that seemed to not want to quit. It was only a small request from Sera. Going with her to Harold Acker's would barely start to repay the huge debt Edie owed her. "Yes, I will come. It'll take me a few moments to get ready." It was just a small thank you from Edie to Sera.

Sera joined Phil in the living room while Edie changed clothes. From the bedroom, she heard Phil thank Sera.

TEN

EDIE AND SERA walked together into the village, through puddles of melting snow, slush, and snow. In normal times, she would have run on the road to Harold's place. And, she estimated, it would have taken her maybe three minutes to run to Harold's house, possibly only five to walk there. But she had Sera to consider. And Sera was carrying a picnic basket. Edie watched Sera carefully negotiate the patches of ice, then took the picnic basket from Sera and offered Sera her arm as support. "This is heavy. What do you have in here?"

"Harold's food for the next few days. It's my turn to see that he has some decent meals."

"Really? How many women are fixing him food?"

"Don't know, it changes with the seasons. Me and a few other women in the congregation are the regulars. We've been taking turns since his wife died."

"Very nice of you."

"It's what we do, look after each other. But we do it more for the memory of our friend Mamie."

They stood by the empty corner store, looked up and down the rural highway—no cars in sight—then crossed over to the other side and turned left.

"Haven't seen Phil's mother around for a while," said Sera.

"That's because I'm not dying."

"What?"

"She's not coming anymore because I'm not dying."

"You weren't dying, you were recovering."

"I think she hoped I was dying. She was disappointed."

"She isn't that bad."

"You don't know her. She's even stopped asking when Phil and I are getting married."

"May I ask why?"

"Because I can't fulfill my duty as a woman."

"What is that duty?"

"Giving Phil . . . God is that an awful phrase. To stop my hemorrhaging, the surgeons removed my uterus. If Phil were to marry me, there's no chance to have a son to carry on the Best name."

"Did she say that to your face?"

"No, to Phil's."

"She should move into the twenty-first century."

"Along with her son," Edie said.

"If he's that backward, why stay with him?"

"It's a mystery to me." She didn't tell Sera that there were times when she looked into Phil's blue eyes and the world melted away—that part of her life no one needed to know. Edie looked up from negotiating the sidewalk covered with ice and other snowy crap; it wasn't much farther to Harold's house, a short block.

"You know when the minister spoke to me after church, I thought he was concerned only about Harold," Sera said.

"What do you think now?"

"That maybe he was concerned about today's collection."

"Why do you think that?"

"The church was half full today, usually it's overflowing. Maybe the snowstorm kept them at home; more likely it was because everyone knew that Harold wouldn't be in church to flash his know-it-all, shit-eating grin at everyone who frequents the bars in Lower Bottom."

"So, you're the one who is concerned about Harold."

"I'm not alone. Since Mamie died, we watch over him for her."

"But mostly you."

"Me and the rest of Troutbeck."

Their conversation ended at Harold's driveway. Edie followed Sera into the breezeway connecting the garage and the house. From what Edie could see, no one ever used the front door, and there wasn't a sidewalk leading to it. Sera knocked, opened the door, and then entered the house as she called out. "Harold, it's me, Sera. I've brought lunch, and a visitor." Edie and Sera took their boots off in the entryway. The house was dark. The shades were pulled past their windowsill. The curtains were closed. There was a musty smell to the house, as if windows and doors had been closed for years. Sera put the basket on the kitchen counter and then turned on the room lights as she went from the kitchen to living room. "Harold, where are you?" Edie followed her into the living room. It was darker than the kitchen. Harold was sitting in his recliner, still in his pajamas. "Harold, did you have anything to eat this morning?" Sera asked.

Harold said nothing.

"I'll put some food on a plate and bring it out to you." Sera went back to the kitchen.

After Edie's eyes adjusted to the dark, she looked around the room. In a corner was a TV set on a table, opposite the picture window was a couch, in front of the couch was a coffee table, and next to Harold was an armchair covered in white fabric with sprays of lavender, a very feminine pattern. The only thing that surprised was the unoccupied armchair. Edie pulled that chair closer to Harold. "Harold, I'm Edie Swift."

"I know who you are."

"It's dark in here, may I open the curtains?" There was no response. Edie opened the picture window curtains. Light flooded in. Edie stared out the window for a moment. So this was the infamous window where Harold could see all the police action on the weekends, thought Edie. She was impressed. "Hope you don't mind, it's been a long, cloudy winter, and I like to soak in the sunshine when I can. Edie pulled the chair even closer to Harold. "I live—"

"I know where you live. You're that detective."

"That's right. I work for the Dane County Sheriff's Office."

"Have they caught the asshole who tried to kill you?"

His bluntness startled Edie. Everyone else used euphemisms for that night and her struggle to not die. She often wondered why. Were they doing that to keep her or them from realizing she had been dancing with death near the abyss? Edie never figured that one out.

"Only the young people."

"Hope they catch the rest of them SOBs."

Edie had never resorted to prayer before, at least not that she could remember, but now she added a silent one. *So do I. So do I. Please.*

Sera placed a tray of food and a cup of coffee on the coffee table. "Harold, you need to eat." Sera handed the cup to Harold. He ignored her. Sera placed the cup back on the tray.

"You going to detect the murder in the cemetery?" Harold asked.

"No, I think Detective Luke Fitzgerald has been assigned to the case."

"I want you."

"It's not up to me. Also, I'm not on duty until to-morrow."

"Then I want you to help that Irish man."

"That's up to my—"

"You tell them bosses I want you. I want those motherfucking assholes who splattered blood all over my Mamie's grave."

Edie changed tactics. "Did you know the victim?"

"Nick Klein? He was a horny little bastard, couldn't leave the women alone. Or maybe it was them that couldn't leave him alone. Surprised he wasn't offed earlier. What's wrong with people today? Doesn't marriage mean anything to them?"

"Everyone missed you at church," said Sera.

"Yeah, sure. It was the minister who missed me. And he missed the money more than me. How much was the collection down?"

"Not my day to count the collection," Sera replied.

"Probably down by more than half. I'll have to get back to church next Sunday or they'll be closing the church for lack of money, then nobody will be looking after my Mamie's grave."

"If you don't eat, you won't make it to church next week," Sera said, placing the tray of food on Harold's lap.

Harold jutted out his jaw, but he ate and sipped the coffee.

While Harold ate, Sera, with Edie's help, cleaned his house. Washed a few loads of clothes. Did the dishes. And fixed a plate of food, which Sera placed in the re-frigerator for Harold's supper. The rest of the food was labeled, dated, and put in the freezer.

Before leaving, Sera went back to the living room, Harold hadn't moved from his chair. "Harold, Edie and I are going now. There's a plate of food in the fridge for your supper. I put the rest of the food in the freezer. Do you remember how to use the microwave?"

"Yeah. Mamie taught me how to punch in the numbers."

"Good, use it to warm your supper. There are some cookies on the kitchen table for a snack. I'll check on you tomorrow."

"Where's that detecting lady?"

"Right here," Edie said, walking into the living room.

"You catch them bastards," Harold ordered.

"I'll do what I can, sir," Edie said.

"Don't try. Do it." Harold turned away from them to watch the road.

"Sweet old man, isn't he?" Edie said when she and Sera were walking back home.

"No, but somehow he got the sweetest woman in the world. I think he knows he hit the jackpot with Mamie, at least I hope he does," said Sera. "I hope whoever did this terrible thing is caught."

"I hope Harold knows that I'm not a miracle worker and probably won't have anything to do with this investigation."

ELEVEN

THE DISHES AT Edie's house were done, the kitchen clean, the baby was sleeping safely in her crib, there was nothing else for Edie to do, and she was antsy. Her energy level was high, but there was nowhere to go and nothing left to do. She flopped on the couch next to Phil; the show he was watching was boring. The book she started yesterday dragged. The energy surging from Edie hit Phil as he watched TV.

He clicked through the satellite channels, couldn't settle on anything to watch. He walked to the kitchen and came back with a beer. He checked on Hillary, she was sleeping. And, finally, he confronted the source of his jumpiness—Edie. "You're making me nervous. Why don't you go for a run?"

"Not good to exercise this close to bedtime."

"Then walk, do something, anything that doesn't involve being in the house."

"Are you kicking me out?"

"Yes. I'd like to relax before I go to bed."

"The honeymoon's over!"

"You need a wedding to have a honeymoon. Please, get out of here, wear off some of your energy before it infects Hillary and wakes her up."

That made sense to Edie; she grabbed a jacket, laced up her running shoes, and stepped through the open door.

"You forgot your cell phone," Phil said as he handed it to her, and then he slammed the door behind her.

She stood alone in the dark. Her stomach began to knot up. The fear had come once more to steal away her resolve. Soon she would be a quivering mass seeking refuge in her bedroom. But from some deep recess of her brain came the notes of "Yankee Doodle." She began to hum that old tune. She took a deep cleansing breath and stepped off her porch. She looked north into the empty farm country. She wasn't ready to take that on tonight. She turned toward Troutbeck.

At Sera Voss's driveway, she met a young girl dressed all in black from her head to her toes. The girl wore a watch cap and balaclava, a snowmobile suit, snowmobile gloves, and boots. A bundle of something was tucked under her arm.

"Hi, Mrs. Best."

"And you are?" said Edie, jogging in place.

"Matilda VandenHuevel, the babysitter of Troutbeck. My mom said you might become one of my clients."

"Potential client. People speak highly of you."

"There's no one to compare me to. I've got a monopoly. I'm the only teenager of babysitting age within a mile of this village. Saw you the other night."

"Which night was that?"

"It's the night I stayed in . . . Friday, the night it snowed. I wanted to go out, but it was cold, the wind felt like a winter storm was on its way. You were whistling "Yankee Doodle" when you ran past my house. My friends and I only sing that when we want to get a tune out of our heads."

Edie was glad to know her precautions on Friday night weren't for nothing "Same here, it works. What are you doing out?"

"Heading north out of the lights of Troutbeck to see the stars."

What lights? Edie thought. "Do your parents know you're out?"

"They should, I do this every chance I get. Can't wait for summer, so I can do it every night and maybe take Sage with me."

"Do your parents know that you wander the farm fields of Troutbeck at night? And who is Sage?"

"Sage is my cousin, and they never ask."

"Aren't you scared of being out in the fields alone?"

"What's there to be afraid of in Troutbeck?"

Edie would have agreed with Matilda last Thursday. Today she didn't know. "Which stars are you looking for tonight?"

"I'm actually looking for constellations; its Boötes turn tonight."

"Know nothing about that."

"Me neither, like, that's why I'm searching for it."

Edie smiled; there was that perennial teen word "like," and there was also the eagerness to know, and the willingness to follow their curiosity. "You know it might be muddy out in the fields?"

"Yeah, but probably not so much on a cold, clear night like this, more likely to be frozen. I came prepared. I've got a tarp, a blanket, a star map, and a flashlight."

Edie admired the girl's preparedness. "Can you stop by sometime this week so we can talk about you babysitting for me?"

"Need to check my schedule first. I'll have Mom call you. See you," Matilda said, readjusting her blanket roll firmly under her arm and heading to the field beyond Edie's house—out of the lights.

Edie stood watch as Matilda walked past Edie's house and into the field. She made a mental note to watch for Matilda each night.

Edie continued her slow jog into Troutbeck, whistling "Yankee Doodle" as she went. Third time through the village she noticed Carole sitting on her porch, wrapped in a blanket, sipping something from a tall mug.

Edie jogged over to her. "What you drinking?"

"Water. What's that tune you were whistling?"

" 'Yankee Doodle'—can't get it out of my head. Are you sure that's really only water?"

"Yup, drink eight glasses a day. It's good for you, want some?"

"Tempting, but I'll wait until I get home."

"Looks like you need a little sprucing up for your first day back tomorrow."

"Don't have any money on me."

"You never do, I'll put it on your tab."

Edie followed Carole through her house and into the salon, settling into the chair at the wash station. The warm water and head massage released stress that Edie didn't know was there.

"Met Matilda tonight," Edie said.

"What constellation is she looking for tonight?"

"You know about her wanderings!"

"Yeah, winter nights are long out here, a girl's got to do something. I'm surprised she's out tonight. She's usually not out on a school night. Heard you went to see Harold Acker. What did he want?"

"That didn't take long to get around town. He wanted me to catch whoever desecrated his wife's grave."

"Are you going to take it on?"

"Can't, probably not, there's no chance of it being assigned to me. Did you also hear I was at the gas station?"

"Hero of the day. What did those gossips over there have to say?"

"One of the men had nothing good to say about Mariah."

"I'll bet it was Nick's brother Jay. Mariah took away his sidekick and he's been angry about it ever since. What else did you find out?"

"Nothing."

"I doubt that. Need to clip a few hairs and then you are done. Tell Phil to keep his hands off my masterpiece, and use a satin pillowcase tonight. I don't want my work ruined."

"Carole?"

"You need something else?"

"Should I go or should I stay?"

"Where did that come from? You should go home."

"That's not what I meant. Phil thinks that I should quit work. He says that he's making enough to support the three of us."

"You got that promise in writing? And I mean a watertight legal document."

"No. We've talked about it, that's all the further it's gone. You know how it goes."

"My advice, don't quit. At least till you got that promise of support in writing. I'm surprised you'd consider quitting, thought you loved your job. Unless you want to quit. Do you want to quit?"

"For the first time since I became a cop, I don't know."

"Being away from work does give you a different perspective on life."

"It seems as if I've been going full-tilt my whole life. Once I made a decision, I never stopped to wonder where I was going or why. But I hit a brick wall last fall, and now that's the only thing I could do this winter—wonder where I was heading and why."

"I thought the brick wall hit you. What have you figured out?"

"Nothing."

"So, do you go, or do you stay?"

"I don't know."

"So, you're going with the flow? That doesn't sound like you. Maybe you need more time to think." Carole snipped the last stray hairs. "I'm done. Need a ride home?'

"No, thanks, I'll walk."

Edie stepped into the chilly, star-filled night. Soon she was whistling. She walked past her house to the field butting up against her lawn—no Matilda, she must have gone home. Edie looked up at the star-studded sky; there wasn't a single constellation she could name. Maybe someday she told herself; maybe someday I'll check them out with Matilda. Then Edie returned home.

Phil was waiting for her. "What were you doing in the field?'

"Looking for Matilda. How did you know I was in the field?"

"I was waiting for you to come home, and Matilda went home fifteen minutes ago."

"How do you know about Matilda's wanderings?"

"It was a long winter. I spent a lot of nights awake. Every clear night, Matilda was in the field looking at the stars. How's Carole?"

"Fine, she said not to touch my hair."

"Anything else I'm not to touch?"

"Didn't leave instructions about that."

Phil closed the curtains, checked that the front door was locked, and then followed Edie into the bedroom.

TWELVE

EDIE DIDN'T HEAR the alarm clock, but she did smell breakfast. Bleary-eyed, she followed that smell into the kitchen. She sat down at the table and then rested her head on it to catch a few more winks. Phil placed a mug of coffee and a plate of eggs and pancakes in front of her. "Careful, the plate's hot."

"Smells delicious," Edie said, lifting her head to see what Phil had made.

"Nothing's too good for my woman."

"Hear that, Hillary? You've gone from being a baby girl to a woman overnight. Great job jumping over those teen years."

"Edie, you know what I mean," Phil said, picking pancake pieces off the floor that Hillary had dropped. "Want me to pack a lunch for you?"

"No thanks, I'll get something downtown."

"Your loss. I've finished that beginning cookbook and am thinking about tackling French cooking next."

"Trying to fatten me up?"

"French people aren't fat."

"Some are." Edie turned her attention to her food. Yes, indeed, Phil was becoming a good cook. "Need anything from the store for tonight?"

"Milk, check the best by date this time. Otherwise, there's plenty of food left in the freezer. You need to get moving, I'll get Hillary ready for Aunt Jill's."

Phil was waiting at the door for Edie with Hillary in one arm, and the diaper bag in the other. He handed the diaper bag to Edie, and then straightened the collar of her white blouse. "Now you're ready to go. What happened to Carole's masterpiece?"

"I always put it in a ponytail for work. Carole said for you not to touch it, not me. How do I look?"

"Like a million."

"Liar."

Phil followed Edie to the car, buckled Hillary into her car seat, and then waved them off.

Edie sat in her car parked in the central Madison parking ramp, trying to decide whether to get out of the car—or not. She felt for her cell. It was still safe in her pocket. She pulled it out, hit the contacts button, and scrolled down to Gracie's number, tapped it, then stared at it. It would be an easy call, just one tap, saying she wasn't coming in. They probably had her on desk duty, just paper-pushing stuff, and she wasn't really needed today. Edie felt the fear twist around her gut like a python. Soon, she knew, it would begin to squeeze and she would be unable to move, then her breathing would go, then she would curl into a ball and freeze. "No," she screamed, and then pounded the steering wheel, keeping time with her no's. The horn blared. She jumped. The sound brought her back to the here and now. "Edie, you are a fool. It's either you or them. You've got to kick them out of your head or you can run home and hide under your bed until you die." Edie pulled the keys from the ignition, shoved them into the pocket along with her cell, then kicked open her car door.

THIRTEEN

A STRING OF "glad to see you," "good to have you back," a couple of handshakes, and a few slaps on the back accompanied Edie to her desk. And on her desk was a bunch of daisies. They were from Phil: "Glad you made it back. Love, Phil," said the card. How did he know about those moments of doubt she had just been through? Was there some type of wormhole between her and Phil that the universe had created? And those daisies, what were they all about? Were they the cheapest flowers or Phil's way of conceding that spring was here? Or did he know about the daisy necklace she'd found in the cemetery? She didn't remember telling him about it. Was she now talking in her sleep? Or maybe the universe was trying to tell her something? The case wasn't even hers to investigate and it was getting under her skin. But whatever the reason it didn't keep the smile from spreading over her face, and it didn't leave, even when Steve informed her that Gracie wanted to see her in her office.

"The rules haven't changed since you've been gone. If I'm not in my office, neither are you," Gracie said, entering her office. "And you are late."

Edie jumped from her chair. An excuse almost made it to her mouth, before she remembered that Gracie didn't like excuses. Edie shut her mouth.

"Have a seat, Detective," Gracie said, as she sat in her own chair.

Edie sat.

Gracie stared at Edie. Edie returned the stare.

"Have you contacted the peer counseling group?" Gracie asked.

"Been busy."

"Edie, make the time. It's good to talk with someone who's been through a similar struggle."

"What would I learn?"

"That you are not alone, that other cops have been through your struggles. That it's okay to cry. That the swaggering tough men around us cry too."

"I'll keep that mind. What is my assignment today?"

"It's changed," said Gracie, her gaze still fixed on Edie. "Why is it that my detectives are scared of you? Or do they know something I don't?"

This was turning into a good old-fashioned stare down from childhood. Whoever blinked first, lost.

"I don't know what you are talking about, Lieutenant."

"Friday a murder victim was found in the Troutbeck cemetery, in your town. The case was given to Detective Luke Fitzgerald. On his way home, after the autopsy on Saturday, Luke was in a car accident. He's still in the hospital recovering from surgery. At this morning's report, every detective I offered the case to declined the assignment. So . . . are they scared of you, or do they know you investigated the scene on your own?"

Edie kept her eyes fixed on Gracie. If she looked away, she would lose and it would be considered by Gracie an admission of guilt. "Again, Lieutenant, I don't know what you are talking about."

Gracie ended the stare down when she glanced at her schedule. She looked up. "Edie, you are now assigned to the Troutbeck case. The file's on your desk, go see the ME about the autopsy, then check with the scene investigators. Now get out of here . . . I've got work to do, and so do you. Good to see you. Call the peer group."

Edie couldn't keep the bounce out of her walk, or the smile off her face as she left Gracie's office.

Edie read the reports written by Gracie, Luke, and the other deputies who were at the scene. She reviewed the case with the ME, cause of death—gunshot wound from a distance, no other contributing factors, but the drug screen panel was pending. Edie's plan for the day was coming into focus: officially go over the murder site, if it had been released. Interview Mariah Collins and set up an interview time with Jay Klein.

On her way back to her desk to arrange for an interview time with Mariah Collins and Jay Klein, and retrieve her flowers, she bumped into Sadie Carpenter.

"Hear the lieutenant handed you the Troutbeck case," said Sadie.

"Yes. Have you released the site yet? I'd like to check it out."

"Yes, but why bother looking it over? I assume you ignored the tape and have been all over the site. Maybe we should go back and cast for more shoe prints, probably find yours throughout that cemetery."

"You know what happens when you assume; you make a fool out of you . . ."

Sadie waited a moment for Edie to finish, and then finished for her. "And me."

"Exactly," said Edie, continuing to her desk.

Edie sat in her car, staring at Lake Monona from the ramp as she called Phil. "I've been given the Troutbeck case."

"She would," said Phil.

"You don't sound thrilled." The silence between them was broken by Edie. "Hey, I'm still in Madison, want me to pick up lunch?"

"Sounds good. Don't have a preference for lunch, get me whatever."

Phil's rotten attitude could not diminish Edie's enthusiasm. The case was hers. She was back in the world. She looked down at her daisies. They reminded her of the daisy necklace she found in the cemetery on Friday night. What was she doing in a parking ramp arranging lunch? She was burning daylight.

FOURTEEN

THERE WAS A deputy sheriff's squad car parked in front of Phil's shop when Edie drove in. Phil was leaning against it talking to Deputy Johnson. She saw that Phil's shop had been tagged—it wasn't even good work. There was no theme, no definition, just big monochromatic scrawls. Didn't anyone take pride in their work anymore? When you have a canvas that big, you should want your best work on display, Edie thought as she joined Phil and Deputy Johnson as they stood outside in the slush looking at the bay doors.

"Edie, you working this case?" Johnson asked.

"No, I'm having lunch with Phil. I've been given the Troutbeck cemetery case. What happened here?"

"Just got here myself. Looks like the building got tagged," said Johnson. "Don't know if the tags mean anything. I've taken pictures and will have the gang unit look at them. I've never seen anything like this, the tags are so huge. I may even ask one of the gangs units to stop out here to have a look in person, see what they can make of it."

"Like I've been saying, it happened because it's spring," said Phil. "It happens to someone every spring, this year it's my turn. It's probably kids just letting off steam that's been pent up over the winter."

"Don't know about that, sir. But this is going to cost you a pretty penny to clean it up. If we can find out who did this, and then get a conviction, maybe you can recoup that cost. So . . . don't do anything until someone from Gangs sees this. Okay?" said Johnson.

"Whatever you say, but make it fast," said Phil. "This is ugly. I want it off my building today."

Edie and Phil waited until Johnson left to talk.

"This is not your case, leave this to Deputy Johnson," said Phil.

Edie couldn't believe what he just said. Phil was refusing to let an experienced detective investigate on her free time and at no cost to anyone. He didn't know what he was missing. "Don't worry, I'll be busy elsewhere."

"Good. I expected you back sooner," said Phil.

"Couldn't get here any sooner—long line for lunch. I can see how your day is now. Did it start any better than this?" Edie asked.

"No. That car you said I'd tow was dug in deep. When I came to get chains to pull it out, I saw this," said Phil.

"Too bad the snow is melting, might have been tracks to give the deputy something to go on."

"Only saw snowmobile tracks, in and out of here. This is a great place to do donuts."

"Any idea who might have done this?" Edie asked.

"No clue, guessing it's local kids. As I said, it happens to someone every year."

"Really? This happens to someone every year? Why do you think that?"

"Who else would do something like this?" said Phil.

"What are you telling me?"

"Nothing. Tagging buildings is a spring ritual."

"No it isn't. At least not in my experience. How about yours?" Phil turned away from Edie to look at the damage to his building. "Am I reading between the lines correctly that you sprayed graffiti on some building when you were a teenager?"

"The statues of limitations have run out on that case. And we were juveniles. And we only did it once. And nobody caught us."

"I hooked up with a guy who did malicious damage to property as a kid, barely missed a drunken driving charge. Anything else you want to confess?"

"No," Phil said and tried to end Edie's interrogation. "Who do you think might have done this?"

"Now you want me on the case. Maybe it was a disgruntled employee—"

"Haven't had any reason to talk to or fire anyone."

"Rival trucking company?"

"Doubtful. I've heard everyone's got all the business they can handle without pushing other companies out."

"Maybe it's some gang wanting to announce itself."

"You'd know that better than me," he said.

"The tags don't look like any gang I know of, but I'm not up on the newest signs. Maybe Acker saw what happened."

"Maybe, he does keep watch over the town. "

"Then again, it might have happened when he was sleeping."

"Leave it to Johnson to ask around. What's your plan for the day?"

"Lunch with you, examine the murder site, talk with the cemetery victim's wife, and set up a time to talk with his brother. Yours?

"Beat on some tire rims to get rid of my frustration, then check the budget, see what I can postpone buying until next year so I can deal with this mess. This is going to cost me a bundle, if my insurance doesn't cover it. I'll be going over my insurance policy to see how much of this is covered, and then talking to my insurance agent. My day's pretty well shot."

"Got any trail cameras on the building?"

"And buy those today."

"Motion detection floodlights?"

"Never needed them before, I'll add that to my list. How much can I borrow from you?"

"Depends on what interest rate you're willing to pay." Carole was right, thought Edie—*don't quit your day job.*

Finn, one of the younger drivers Phil employed, walked over. "Sorry to interrupt you, boss, but Max is having problems."

"What is it this time?" Phil asked.

"Had to take some detours and got lost," said Finn.

"He's got a company phone, it has GPS on it. Tell him to use it."

"Claims he keeps losing the signal."

"Okay, I'll be with you in a moment," Phil said, watching as Finn went back to the shop.

"Damn, the disasters are piling up today. With Max lost, and this mess to clean up, all I can afford to pay you, Edie, is my undying gratitude."

"Hmmm, I'll think about it. Can I get that in writing?"

FIFTEEN

THIS TIME, EDIE'S investigation of the scene would be public knowledge. She parked her car in front of the Troutbeck church, then ducked under the police tape in full view of whoever wanted to watch her. When she finished looking at the scene, she'd take the tape down. It was a constant reminder of the human loss to their community, and, with the tape gone, maybe the community could begin to heal.

Edie walked the quarter mile to the cemetery. This time she knew what to expect; she hoped the snowmelt left something to see.

She worked the scene as if she had never been there. Daylight illuminates things that a penlight can't. When Edie finished examining the crime scene, she sat on the bench that Nick Klein had sat on and died. It was still bloody. Even after the snow melted there was blood everywhere. Still she sat where Klein sat and wondered what he had been doing in the cemetery in the middle of the night. Who comes to a cemetery at night besides ghosts, ghouls, and goblins? She wondered if kids still held their breath when passing a cemetery, as some of her friends did years ago. Her mind jumped forward to wondering about who would scrub away the evidence of violent death: the church ladies, Mamie Acker's friends, or Harold Acker, when she took down the tape. Damn. She needed to focus on Klein. She looked down at her pants. There was sure to be blood on the butt—should she wash them or throw them away? Damn. When did she start caring about a pair of pants? What else was she going to change as her years added up?

Edie jumped up from the bench. She was wasting time. Keep the focus on what is in front of you, she told herself. The ME said the shot came from a distance. From the way Klein had fallen, the ME said, and the crime scene investigator agreed, the shot could not have come from the west and the windbreak. It couldn't have come from the south because of the knoll—any shot from there would have caused more damage, and it was the wrong angle. Not from the north either; the church and the village were there, and someone would have complained of gunfire within the village limits. That left the south, the same conclusion she had Friday night. Edie turned to survey that direction. There was a farmhouse, fields, and a stand of trees some distance from the farm. The report wasn't clear on whether that area had been checked. She'd talk with Johnson and Smith about it. Possibly bring in a K-9 unit, if the snow hadn't masked any scent or washed it away. No harm in asking.

Edie turned her focus back to the cemetery. She read Mamie Acker's headstone: Mamie Karl Acker, Beloved Wife of Harold Acker. Hard to believe that foul-mouthed, cantankerous man had a soft side, thought Edie. Mamie must have been a saint. Mamie's stone reminded her of another Mamie. She followed the row of Acker gravestones to the west until she found the other Mamie.

A car backfiring dropped Edie to the ground. She picked herself off the ground, wiped off what mud she could, brushed water, twigs, and grass from her clothes, and looked around to see if anyone noticed her sprawled in the mud. Enough of this. The town's peace had been broken, she had work to do.

Edie read the headstone of the other Mamie: Mamie Robin Neuport Brown, Beloved Wife of Thomas Brown, Gone Too Soon, In Our Hearts Forever. "What happened to you?" Edie asked the headstone. It was silent. She hoped the living would be more talkative. She pulled out a notebook, wrote down Mamie Robin's vitals, wondered who might know what happened to her—maybe the historian. Putting her notebook away, she squatted in front of the headstone and looked for the place where she had last seen the daisy necklace. The melting snow had washed away the gritty soil and moved it inches from where she had found it on Friday night. Edie pulled an evidence bag from her pocket, put on her vinyl gloves, then placed the necklace into the bag, labeled it, signed it, then carefully placed it in the inside pocket of her jacket. She'd hand it over to over to Sadie later.

Edie walked up the knoll for a better view. From there, the high point of the area, the country spread at her feet. For all its flatness, there was beauty in this country, and peace. Edie wondered if that broad expansive view of the land was why the cemetery was placed there. Those pioneers had grubbed in the dirt all their lives. Ditched the land in order to drain. Built barns for their livestock before raising decent shelter for their families. Was this piece of land meant to be an eternal lookout of the land for those pioneers who had worked it until they died? Was this cemetery the land promised to those pioneers when they were done with their rough-and-tumble life?

Edie rocked back and forth on her feet as she brainstormed various scenarios of what had happened here.

Daylight confirmed what she had seen by flashlight on Friday night; there wasn't much to see. Edie walked through the cemetery, a mix of new and old graves. She stopped in front of one old headstone; the children of the family were listed: Johann, Anna, Michel, Michel, and Michel—how strange to have so many children named Michel. What was that all about? Was this stone tall because the family wanted to pierce the heavens and direct the angels' tears to where their Michels lay? Reading the stones, Edie saw that many of the last names repeated themselves throughout the cemetery and that they could still be heard in Troutbeck today. This was a new home built by people who had left their native lands, crossing oceans and mountains, and from which their less adventuresome ancestors had not strayed too far. Why? she wondered.

Troutbeck began to jell for Edie as she read the grave markers. It was a tight-knit Bavarian community that closed itself off during The Great War meant to end all wars, and they pulled in any leftover welcome mats in after World War II. From what she knew of the town from her short residency, the town would fit nicely in Brigadoon, thought Edie. One more thing to ask the historian about. But not today. The rest of the day would be given to interviewing the young, grieving widow, Mariah Collins.

SIXTEEN

ON EDIE'S FIRST glance, Nicholas' and Mariah's place was stark. No frills. It was a monument to work. An old, square, two-story farmhouse with a stone foundation that had been remodeled into two apartments. Access to the second floor was from a rickety-looking outside staircase that probably wouldn't pass any house inspection today. It had white vinyl siding with barn red trim, probably from leftover paint from the barn that stood to the right, someone's notion of not wasting anything. The barn was collapsing in on itself but still held some decaying bales of straw. Edie didn't see any farm equipment. Probably wasn't a working farm, at least by the current occupants of the buildings.

Edie parked her car in the drive, walked to what looked like the front door, then knocked, loudly. Waited. No response. She knocked, again. No response. Edie checked her watch, she was a little early, and so she walked back to her car and leaned against it, soaking in the warmth of the spring day. Moments later, at the appointed time, she knocked again. This time Edie heard footsteps coming to the door—success.

Her wrinkled clothes, the hair that needed combing, suggested that Mariah Collins had been sleeping, but the red eyes and puffy face indicated she had been crying.

She looked pale to Edie; maybe it was her dark hair that emphasized Mariah's winter skin.

"Mariah Collins?" Edie asked.

"That's me," she replied.

"I'm Detective Swift; I've been assigned to your husband's case."

"What happened to the other detective?"

"He's on medical leave. May I come in?"

"Sure. Sorry about the mess. I haven't been able to pull myself together since that day. It's a wonder that I can plan his funeral. Thank God for rituals."

Edie followed Mariah into the kitchen. A Formica-topped table, with chairs to match, sat in the middle of the room. Dirty dishes were piled next to the sink. Mariah cleared a bowl of half eaten cereal and two carry-out boxes with food barely touched from the table, dumping them into the trash. Mariah sat down, put her arms on the table, and then rested her head on them.

"Mariah, are you okay?" Edie asked.

"I think so. I'm just tired all the time. Can't sleep at night, can barely stay awake during the day. I didn't know it would be this tough."

"Maybe you should see a doctor?"

"I've got too much to do before Nick's funeral." Tears flowed down Mariah's cheeks.

Edie looked for a box of tissue, didn't see anything. She ripped off a section of paper towels that she spied behind the stacks of dirty dishes on the counter. She handed it to Mariah. "Do you have family to help you?"

"None in the immediate area. My family lives in La Crosse. My parents are out of the area; they can't make it until later in the week and I don't want Nick's family here. I'm glad his family can't come. It's bad enough having to spend time with them this weekend at the visitation and funeral. I'm sorry, please, have a seat."

Edie sat across the table from Mariah and let her ramble.

"They don't like me, never did, wanted him to marry someone from the neighborhood, anyone. It would have been easier for them to step on a girl who accepted the culture of the area, and grind her to dust, like they tried to do with me. And they talk about the Irish being clannish! Well . . . fuck them all!" Mariah buried her head in her arms and cried.

Edie sat quietly. She knew not to interrupt someone who was spilling their guts, though she did take notes. She looked at her watch, only three hours until she had to pick up Hillary. Maybe when Mariah's ramblings slowed she could ask to use the bathroom and while there she would call Aunt Jill and beg her to drive Hillary home. Edie wanted to finish this interview today, even if it was made longer by bouts of tears and moans.

"I'm so sorry, but I seem to be crying a lot these days. Once I start, I can't stop," Mariah said, brushing tears from her cheeks.

"Understandable. This has been a terrible few days for you, and no one to share them with you. Is this a good place to talk? Maybe we can go to the living room. It might be more comfortable for you."

Mariah looked around her kitchen. "I'd rather talk here. It's more comfortable, and the rest of the house is in worse shape. I'm kinda hungry, do you mind if I eat? Would you like something to eat, or drink?"

Edie looked around at the mess. "No thanks. Please, find yourself something to eat." She thought it might be better if Mariah didn't eat until the kitchen had been cleaned.

Mariah pulled a box of crackers from a cupboard, poured some in a bowl, and then began to nibble her way through them.

Edie started the interview when Mariah returned to the table.

"First of all, I'm sorry about your husband's death."

"Thank you."

"And, under these circumstances, there is no good time to ask questions."

"Go ahead."

"How long were you married to Nick?"

"Four years, a few too many."

"Have you always lived here?"

"Sort of, we used to have the upstairs when his grandmother was alive. When she died, we moved down here. We wanted to fix this place up. Nick started to make this a single-family home before . . ." Mariah wiped the tears away. "We had an agreement with his family to buy this place."

"Do you plan on staying here?"

"Not anymore. This place needs more work than I could do myself, or that I can pay to have done. Nick was going to do all the work." Mariah chuckled a few times. "Would serve his family right if I made them live up to the agreement and kept the place. But I don't want to be anywhere near them."

"Why is that?"

"Did you know that we are sitting on sacred ground to the Klein family, and they would like to keep it in the family, and I am not family. Never was. I could never figure out why that was. Maybe because I didn't take their name, or maybe because I took their precious boy away from them. I don't know."

Edie looked around the kitchen and beyond the messiness. She guessed the room hadn't been remodeled since the fifties and then it was only a haphazard update. And if the kitchen, the central gathering place in any house, was dilapidated, the rest of the house probably was too. She agreed with Mariah that it was a dump; only a bulldozer could improve the place. "Is there some reason Nick's family doesn't like you?"

"They're morons."

"Did they all dislike you, or was it just one person?" Edie wanted to explore this thread of their conversation until it didn't pan out anymore.

"Don't really know. Jay seemed to be their spokesperson. They followed his lead."

"What do you know about Jay?"

"Before Nick and I got married we'd all hang out, but after the wedding, he didn't want anything to do with me. Did you know that at our wedding that asshole took a picture of my ass as I was getting into the backseat of a two-door car, and then sent it to Nick. Do you know how big my ass looked in a wedding dress? Who does that stuff? The asshole, moron."

Edie let the widow rant on. Better to let Mariah blow off steam in words than actions. "Could I get a list of Nick's friends and relatives?"

"Sure, at least the male friends. I don't know who the female friends were, and after a while, I didn't care."

"What do you mean?"

Mariah took a deep breath, "My husband was a . . . was a . . . what's the male equivalent of a slut?"

Edie didn't know, she'd never been asked that question. She mentally reviewed a few of the domestic disturbance cases she had responded to which had expanded her vocabulary considerably, but had never heard the word for a male slut. "No idea."

"Last year I'd found out he was sleeping with Ashley Zelinski, told him to shape up or he was out. Then I learned there were others before her."

"You stayed with him."

"Yeah, stupid me. But when he wasn't chasing ass, he was the sweetest person I ever knew."

"Did he stop chasing women after you found out?"

Mariah hesitated. "After I confronted him, yes, until recently."

"How do you know that?"

"The usual. He kept different hours at work, stayed out late, extra nice to me, bought me flowers and jewelry, and I smelled someone else's perfume on his clothes."

"Did you recognize the scent?"

"It smelled like something my cousin wore when she was young. I'm pretty sure he wasn't sleeping with my cousin."

"How do you know that?"

"That cousin lives in the Twin Cities."

"What did you do then?"

"Told him to get out, I was filing for divorce."

"When was that?'

"Thursday night. If I hadn't kicked him out, maybe he'd be alive." Mariah began to cry, again. "Did I send him to his death?"

Edie hoped that her legendary poker face hadn't taken a hiatus. The spouse was usually the first person of interest, and the passion that brought two people together often was a two-sided coin. And nothing Mariah said had eliminated her from that position.

"Mariah, do you have a gun?"

"No. You think I killed him?"

"It is a standard question. Did Nick own a gun?"

"No. The only time he went hunting was with his friend Lee Mitchell, and Lee would loan him one."

"Mariah, what were you doing the night of Nick Klein's death?"

"Besides kicking him out? Sleeping."

"Can anyone confirm that?"

"Not that I can think of. How many people do you know who kick their husband out of the house and their life in front of a crowd?"

"Do you know of anyone who wanted to hurt Nick?"

"No one, everyone liked Nick."

Except one, thought Edie—you.

"Could I get the list of friends and relatives before I leave, and may I use your bathroom?"

"Sure, the bathroom's down that hallway, then to the right. I'll start on that list."

Edie perched on the edge of the tub as she made her call to Aunt Jill about being late.

"Don't worry, sweetie. Hank's invited me for dinner. I'll drop Hillary off at your house on the way to Hank's."

What the hell did Hank Erb want with her aunt? After this case was over, she promised herself to find out. It took Edie a few moments to regain her composure and reconnect with the murder investigation. When she calmed down, she flushed the toilet to continue the pretense, took a closer look at the bathroom—yup, it was like the rest of the house. If the house wasn't bulldozed, it was going to be someone's money pit.

SEVENTEEN

EDIE HAD BEEN informed that Sadie Carpenter had the Klein evidence. Putting the necklace into evidence should have been easy, but this could get complicated. Edie fortified herself with a couple of deep breaths, put a smile on her face, and went looking for Sadie.

Edie stood in front of Sadie's desk, holding out the packet containing the necklace.

"What is that?" Sadie asked.

"A necklace I found at the Troutbeck cemetery, near the crime scene, when I went over the site this afternoon," Edie replied.

"Where did you find it?"

"Approximately twenty-five feet from the bench where the body was found. Saw something sparkle in the sun on the gravel road. I investigated and found this," said Edie.

"Any relevance to the crime?"

"I don't know. I want it in the evidence box because I found it near the scene."

"Why didn't my people find it?"

"Again, I don't know. Ask them."

"May I see it?"

Edie handed the bag over to Sadie. While Sadie looked at the necklace, she filled out the chain of custody paperwork.

"It looks old, could have been in the cemetery a long time. Probably dropped there years ago," said Sadie.

"That is a possibility. Why are you making this hard? I looked over the scene. I found this necklace. Now I am entering it into the evidence box. What more can I tell you? How the guy was killed? Who killed him? Why it happened?"

"The great Edie Swift should know that by now."

Shit, thought Edie, *isn't it time we drop this rivalry?* Sure, during the police academy, she was always a few steps ahead of Sadie, but they'd been working on the same team and toward the same goal for years—justice for those who didn't know what hit them. *Time to act like it, Sadie.* "That's a great testament to my ability. Maybe that's why I was assigned to the case. So, you do your part, run your tests on the necklace. I'll tell you if it's important after I track down the killer. Okay?"

"Anything the wise and wonderful Swift says. Thought you'd improve with time off."

Edie turned around and left. Well, Sadie hadn't changed during that time, she thought. Somehow, Sadie still knew what buttons of Edie's to push and couldn't resist pushing them. She'd have to suck up Sadie's back-handed insults until she knew if the department's internal politics had changed. All she wanted to do now was to go home and crawl into bed.

EIGHTTEEN

THE DAY'S LINEUP had worn out Edie. She'd have to get used to the long hours and the emotions that were dumped on her by victims. Or on becoming the rock on which everyone's emotions crashed—again. She missed her afternoon naps. Her bed was inviting—she'd crawl into it, pull the covers over her head, and shut everything else out. Like a cave, but comfortable. Slipping under the covers, Edie was glad she had discovered flannel sheets that winter; lying between them was like being on a Florida beach minus the sun and sand—you did what you had to do to get through a Wisconsin winter. But the interviews with Mariah and the images of Aunt Jill spending the day with Hank Erb were playing on an endless loop, preventing her from sleeping. It was well after Phil had joined her in bed that she drifted toward sleep.

"Gunfire!" Edie shouted as she rolled out of bed onto the floor, and started crawling to the closet for her gun. "Get down! Go get Hillary. I'll get my gun."

"No, Edie, that was a car backfiring," Phil said, as he arranged pillows between him and the bed's headboard.

"Are you sure? It sounded like a shot to me."

"That's because you were almost asleep. Believe me, it was a car backfiring."

"They need to get it fixed. Now."

"I'll pass the word. Come back to bed."

"I can't sleep."

"Well, I can't sleep without you. Come keep me company," Phil said in his most seductive voice as he peered over the edge of the bed.

Edie left off the quest for her gun and crawled back to bed. "I'll keep you company, but I don't think I can sleep."

"That's okay. We'll talk all night, if we need to. Your heart is pounding. You're cold." He held her closer, and pulled the blankets around her shoulders.

Edie fell asleep to the steady beat of Phil's heart, and the warmth of his body as it wrapped around hers.

For Phil, it was going to be another long night trying to keep Edie's demons at bay.

NINETEEN

IT WAS MORNING and Edie wasn't in a good mood and last night's car episode hadn't helped it any. She pulled clothes from the closet, and drawers, then threw the discards on the bed. Nothing. Not one piece of clothing was right. After a sedentary winter spent in sweats, there were maternity clothes and the pre-pregnancy clothes before that to choose from . . . nothing was right. And she didn't want to take the time to shop for new clothes. Edie took a deep breath as she surveyed the mess. What the hell was wrong?

She reviewed the morning: It was chilly, but weren't most spring mornings? She and Phil managed to get Hillary through breakfast without having to clean the whole kitchen. And then . . . and then Aunt Jill knocked on Edie's front door. That's what was wrong with the day! Aunt Jill had knocked on the door. Phil had quickly kissed her and Hillary good-bye, grabbed his travel mug of coffee, and run out the door. Aunt Jill picked up Hillary and the diaper bag, kissed Edie good-bye, and then put Hillary in her car seat for the drive back to Madison. No explanations about Aunt Jill's sudden appearance. No time given for Edie to civilly formulate or ask the questions that were building up in her brain. Nothing besides good morning was said. Nothing, no explanations.

Nothing. Edie was left with questions, and a picture of Aunt Jill with a smile that never ended.

Well . . . Edie would wipe that smile off Aunt Jill's face when all the evidence against Henry Erb was gathered. But before she could find out what that evidence might be, she had an interview with Jay Klein. And she didn't have a thing to wear. Damn.

Edie's day wasn't getting any better. She'd picked Crystal Mitchell from Mariah's list to call. Edie kept her emotions in check as Crystal hemmed and hawed about committing to an interview time. But Edie persisted and arranged to meet Crystal and her husband at five that afternoon at their place.

Edie took a break from calling the people on Mariah's list and instead was hanging out at the front desk of the Northeast precinct as she waited for Jay Klein to show. She watched a man get out of a black pickup with flame details on the side, and gleaming chrome pipes and fenders. He looked like the man who had stormed out of the gas station and been identified by other bar patrons and Mike Erdmann as Jay Klein, but she had never been introduced to him and she last saw him at the Troutbeck Bar and Gas with day-old stubble and wearing a snowmobile suit. She estimated the man to be about late thirties, five-foot-eight, thinning black hair, a beer gut. So, men couldn't use clothes to hide their transgressions either. Dressed in blue jeans and T-shirt, the morning chill didn't seem to bother him. As he cleared the rear of the pickup, he squared his shoulders and walked with a swagger the rest of the way to the way to the station. Edie wondered about the swagger. Was he telling the world that he was a tough guy despite his height? Was he hiding uncertainty? Scared? She'd find out soon enough.

She turned her back on the man's performance to talk with the deputy doing desk duty. The door opened, and someone stomped to the desk.

"I've got an appointment with an Edie Swift," said the man.

Edie turned to him, held out her hand, and with her sweetest smile said, "I'm Detective Swift. And you are?"

"I'm Jay Klein," he said, shaking her hand.

Edie judged that his handshake was meant to be overpowering, but Edie hung in there, matching grip for grip. "We'll be using one of the back rooms today for our interview."

Jay released his grip first—Edie won the first round. Was he really tough or acting the part? Edie sized him up, two could play that game. It would be so much easier Edie thought, if they'd think with their brains instead of their penises. "Follow me, please," she said. Edie put a little sway into her walk; a strong handshake, a little hip action, and a swaying ponytail would certainly discombobulate this man. Men were so easy.

Edie sat across the table from Jay Klein, and watched him look around the room.

"Is this where you do it?" Jay asked.

"Do what?"

"Question, no, that's not the word . . . interrogate prisoners. I don't see no cameras. Or any recording devices."

"No, we don't interrogate people here. This is an interview room. You are not under arrest, Mr. Klein. I asked you to come in to talk about your brother, help us to find the murderer. The more you can tell me about him, the better picture I can get about who might have committed this crime. Let's start this out right. Thank you for coming in to talk with me."

"No problem, I want the bitch that did this to my brother."

"Why do you think a woman killed your brother?"

"I don't think. I know. It was that bitch that tricked Nick into marrying him. She couldn't get her Mrs. Degree in La Crosse, had to come to Madison to snag one. Bet she told Nick she was pregnant so he would marry her."

Edie wondered if he was deliberately trying to goad her, or did that stuff naturally fall from his mouth? She mentally counted to ten, and then continued. "Why do you think it was Nick's wife?"

"Ain't it always the spouse?"

"Interesting, I'll keep that assessment in mind. Could you tell me something about your brother?"

"Why? He's dead."

"The more I know about him, the more I might understand why someone wanted him dead."

"Nick was a sweet kid. Always up for a good time. We could count on him. Once he stiffed his fiancée to go snowmobiling with me and Chad. We had a blast that weekend."

"So, he had a date with Mariah Collins—"

"No, his first fiancée."

"Who was that?"

"Holly Sundby."

"Do you have a telephone number or address for her?"

"Why?"

"I'd like to talk to as many of Nick's friends as possible."

"You want their names and numbers, too?"

"Yes, please."

"Shit lady, what do you want me to do, write a book about my brother or something?"

"Nothing that drastic, just some names and numbers will do. Now, getting back to the weekend that you Nick, and Chad . . . Chad who?"

"Chad Bahr, our cousin."

"I'd like his phone and address also, please. So, you, Nick, and Chad Bahr went snowmobiling when Nick was supposed to do something with his fiancée Holly Sundby."

"Yeah, that was a good weekend. Pissed Holly off so much she called off the wedding. Don't understand why she did that. Sometimes that girl was just plain crazy. She got in a mood and she'd blast anything that got in her way. That girl is a crack shot. Always gets her buck on opening day. He dodged the marriage bullet that time. But he jumped into the fire with that current bitch." Jay shrugged his shoulders. "He must've liked them crazy."

"Then what happened?"

"What do you mean? Nick was free, he escaped the ball and chain that time."

"Just trying to get a picture of him. What else can you tell me about your brother?"

"Well . . . he was a good guy. He was a good uncle to my kids."

"Are you married?"

"Had to do right by her."

"Do you and Nick have any other family members?"

"My sister, my parents."

"Would you write their names, telephone numbers, and addresses down for me?" Edie placed a pad of paper and pen in front of Jay. She waited for him to finish writing before she continued. "What can you tell me about Mariah Collins?"

"That bitch had no respect for my brother, calls herself Mariah Collins. I don't know why he married her—she wasn't knocked up or anything. She must've had him by the short hairs."

"Did your brother have a happy marriage?"

"It's marriage, what's happy about it? I know I was happier when he hooked up with Holly again."

"His first fiancée?"

"Yeah."

"When did that happen?"

"A year or so after Nick got married." A chuckle escaped from Jay.

"Where is Holly living now?"

"Sun Prairie."

"Got an address for her?"

"No. And she didn't do it."

"Not accusing her of anything, just one more person to get a better picture of your brother's life. You mentioned a cousin Chad—"

"Chad Bahr."

"Do you have an address for him?"

"Madison."

It was time to end this interview; Jay Klein wasn't going to give her much more information about Nick, thought Edie. "Can you think of anyone who wanted to harm Nick?"

"No, you'd have to ask the girls in his life."

"Do you know their names?"

"Nope, I just sat back and watched him have fun."

"Mr. Klein, this is a standard question: where were you the night of your brother's death?"

Jay looked astonished at the question. "I didn't do it. I was at home with the wife and kids."

"And your wife will confirm that?"

"Yeah."

Edie stood up. "Jay, thank you for coming in. I'll show you the way out." She held the door for him, and then followed him down the corridor. "One more thing. I was wondering how Mariah and Nick met."

"Blind date, not long after Holly called off the wedding. You'll pass on to the head detective that I think Mariah did it?"

"No need to, I'm investigating this case."

"You! This ain't gonna be good. I thought someone with balls was on the case."

"I am a detective and I will do my best to solve this case. You've got my card, please call me if you think of anything else that might concern this case."

"Stop jabbering, and wasting my money, woman. Arrest Mariah, she done it." He swaggered out of the precinct.

After Jay left the building, laughter erupted from the deputies who were standing around the front desk and had overheard the exchange between Edie and Jay. "Gotta tell that one at report tonight. The word on the street is that Edie Swift has no balls."

"No one believes that, Dougie. My balls are bigger and visible," said Edie as she cupped her breasts and gave them a gentle lift up. "Let's see yours." She walked back to the interview room to write her report in quiet. What she really needed was a shower to wash all the shit that had been thrown around during the interview.

It really wasn't her day. There were no lights on at Crystal's house when she arrived at the agreed-upon time. No one answered the knock on the door, or the doorbell, or the phone. Edie checked her watch, it was after five, close to suppertime. She walked around the house, no cars in the drive, no visible disturbance; she finally put her business card in the door with a note to please call. Damn, it was time that she was home, she'd have to catch Crystal another time and place.

TWENTY

HOW RIDICULOUS TO be wearing a winter coat on a spring morning. Winter is over and spring should get its act together, Edie thought as she flipped up her coat collar, then wrapped her wool-gloved hands around her coffee cup, waiting in the retreating night for Crystal Mitchell's shift to end. And, while she waited, she mulled over Aunt Jill and that man Hank Erb.

She had to admit that Aunt Jill hooking up with Hank Erb was a shock. She couldn't remember Aunt Jill introducing any man to her as she was growing up. Maybe there never were any men in her aunt's life. If that was the case, what did Aunt Jill know about men? Did Aunt Jill know how to act around them? And if they were doing IT, were they taking precautions? Aunt Jill was past the age to get pregnant, but HIV, herpes, and other STDs—my God, she'd have to sit Aunt Jill down and have THE talk! Through her mental ramblings, Edie kept an eye on the nursing home, expecting Crystal Mitchell to walk out of the nursing home at any minute.

Edie blocked out the thoughts of her aunt when she saw a small gaggle of women leave the building. They walked in a bunch. She couldn't tell which one was Crystal until the women started to peel off from the group toward their car.

Crystal walked out of work with her head down. She wore a long, shapeless winter coat, high winter boots—nothing that would distinguish her from the women who had just left her. She lifted her head as she neared her car. She stopped. Edie could see that Crystal recognized her. And Edie stood between her and her car. There was nothing left for Crystal to do but put a smile on her face.

"Detective Swift," said Crystal, "what are you doing here?"

"Things didn't work out last night."

"Sorry, I forgot the time," said Crystal, loosening a chunk of asphalt with her toes.

"Thought this might be a better time, fit into both our schedules. Is this an okay place to talk?" Edie wanted this interview. Crystal Mitchell was Mariah's closest friend. You went where the information was, even if it meant getting up before the crack of dawn to get it . . . and standing in the cold.

"In the parking lot?"

"Yes. Are you okay with it?"

"Works for me."

"Care for a cup of coffee? Brought an extra cup along."

"No, thanks. Don't drink the stuff this early in the morning, it'll keep me awake. I usually go home and sleep after work."

"From our phone call yesterday, I thought that might be the case. How's the car?"

"Getting worked on. Mariah's been loaning me hers to get to work."

"What's Mariah doing for a car?"

"We're trading off using it. I use it to get to and from work at night, and she gets it the rest of the day. Luckily, she's not very busy these days. Oh, that isn't lucky, is it?"

"She sounds like a good friend."

"What did you want to ask me?" Crystal shifted her weight from one foot to the other to keep warm.

"I'm trying to get a picture of Nick Klein. How well did you know him?"

Crystal pulled up her coat's hood and stuffed her hands into her coat pockets. "Not much, he was more Lee's friend than mine."

"Who is Lee?'

"My husband. He and Nick were friends in high school. Ever since his death I've been trying to remember what year Nick was in, he wasn't in mine."

"Know of anyone who had a grudge against Nick?"

"No," Crystal said staring at the piece of asphalt she had finally worked loose from one of the many potholes in the parking lot. "You'd have to ask Lee, he'd know more than me."

"How do I get in touch with Lee?" Silence. Edie had hit a wall. Maybe she should have talked with Crystal downtown, she thought. Would a formal setting have made a difference for this mousy woman? Edie shrugged her shoulders, who knew? You go where you need to get the information. "Do I remember correctly that Lee went on a turkey hunt this past weekend?"

"Yes," Crystal said to the parking lot.

"Is he back?"

"Yes," Crystal whispered.

"Can I reach him at home, or at work?"

"He works nights, like me. Lee doesn't like to be disturbed at work. He says it takes too long for him to get back into working."

"Where does he work?"

"At the truck place near the interstate."

"If he can't be interviewed at work, may I stop by your house so I can talk with Lee?"

"This hasn't been a good week for Lee; he's taking Nick's death really hard."

"Sorry to hear that." Edie waited. She was experienced at the silence game.

"Best to come at suppertime."

"That didn't work last night. Is there a better time for Lee?"

"I don't know. I'll have to ask Lee."

"That would be nice of you." Edie pulled out her business card and handed it to Crystal. "You or Lee can call me at that number." Edie doubted that she'd get a call; plan B was to talk with him at work, and if that didn't work, she'd punt.

Crystal took the card, looked at it, and then stuffed it in her coat pocket.

TWENTY-ONE

EDIE WROTE UP a report on her morning talk with Crystal Mitchell as she waited for her next interview, Holly Sundby. Maybe that talk with Crystal should've been here, four walls, no prying eyes, and no place for her to hide, thought Edie.

Edie felt a current of energy ripple through the office; she walked to the front to investigate the disturbance. A pretty blonde, of course, standing at the front desk, seemed to be the focus of everyone's attention. Petite, blue jeans tucked into cowboy boots, blue jean jacket that ended at the waist, the blonde hair cascading down her back stopping just above her butt. Edie guessed the woman was in her late twenties, maybe early thirties.

"I have an appointment with a Detective Swift," said the pretty lady when she walked up to the front desk.

Edie watched all the men rush to assist the damsel in distress. Finally, one of the deputies won whatever contest had been going on between the men and got to escort her to Edie.

"Hello, I'm Detective Swift, and you are?"

"Holly Sundby."

They shook hands. Decent handshake for someone so petite, blonde, and helpless looking, thought Edie.

"Thanks for coming in, we'll go to an interview room where we can talk in private." Edie lead the procession of Holly and the deputy to the interview room

Holly stood by the chair across from Edie. *What was she waiting for? Me to pull the chair out for her?* thought Edie. A few seconds later the deputy did just that, and then stepped back against the wall.

"Thank you, deputy, but Ms. Sundby and I will be talking privately."

"Thought I'd stay here in case you needed anything," said the deputy.

"Could I have some water?" asked Holly Sundby, smiling at him.

The deputy was out the door and back in seconds with a bottle of water and a glass filled with ice, which he placed in front of her. "Anything else, ma'am?"

"Why, thank you, no. You are a sweetheart to get this for me," said Holly.

The deputy went back to his post against the wall.

"Thank you, deputy, I'll take it from here," said Edie, escorting him from the room and firmly shutting the door. "Sorry about that."

"Don't be, it happens to me all the time," Holly said with a smile.

I'm sure it does, thought Edie. "Thank you for coming in," said Edie, with a smile. "I have a few questions about Nicholas Klein. I hear that you were once engaged to Mr. Klein."

"That was a long time ago."

"Can you be more specific?"

"I think it was four, maybe five or six years ago, just before Nick married, um . . . um . . . before Nick got married to his current wife."

"Nick was married before?"

"No. Nick and I were only engaged. Luckily, it was called off before any expensive wedding arrangements were made."

"Who called off the wedding?"

"My mother."

"Your mother?"

"Yes, she said I'd be sorry if I married a constant sidekick like Nick."

"What did she mean by that?"

"Nick was at the beck and call of everyone, especially that brother of his. During our engagement, Nick seemed to be gone every weekend. He was either hunting, fishing, or snowmobiling, always something. Hadn't noticed it before we got engaged, we'd all hang out together, I was part of the gang. But once I put a ring on my finger, things changed. It was like I wasn't welcome anymore. I finally listened to my mother and told Nick the wedding was off."

"How did Nick take the cancellation of the wedding?"

"Badly. Wanted his ring back, but it was mine. Had to have something for all the trouble I went through during that engagement. Got it made into a necklace. Pretty isn't it?" Holly said, pulling a diamond pendant from between her breast to show Edie. "Next thing I knew, he was engaged, again."

"What was your reaction to his new engagement?"

"I felt free. He wasn't my concern anymore. I no longer sat in my apartment thinking about what might have been with Nick. Or waiting for him."

"Do you know of anyone who had a grudge against Nick?"

"No, he was a sweet guy. But I did dodge a bullet there."

"Why do you say that?"

"After I called off our wedding, I learned Nick was a skirt chaser."

"How did you learn that?"

"I ran into Nick at the mall sometime after his wedding. We arranged to have dinner to talk about old times and see how each of us was doing. That night, after dinner, nature took its course."

"So . . . you were having an affair with Nick while he was married?" *One more person to put on the list of suspects.*

"He was mine, before he was hers."

"Did the affair end?"

"It wasn't an affair, it was only a fling. Lasted a few months, then it kinda petered out."

Edie wondered how long Holly had been waiting to tell that story. "Did you see him after the fling was over?"

"About a year later I bumped into him at the mall, introduced him to the friend I was with. She took it from there."

"What does that mean?"

"I told you Nick was a skirt chaser. She jumped his bones every time her husband and Nick's wife were out of town."

"How long did that affair last?"

"A few months, hmmm, there seems to be a pattern there."

"Does this friend have a name?"

"Ashley Zielinski, but don't contact her when her husband's in town. They have this rule about flings."

"What is that rule?"

"Don't tell, don't ask."

"How long have you known Ashley Zielinski?"

"A while now, can't remember the date. Met her at a shooting range. Boy, can that girl shoot."

"Could you write down Ashley Zielinski's phone and address for me, please?" Edie asked, sliding paper and pen to Holly. "How am I to know when her husband's out of town?" *That's number three and four suspect to put on the suspect list.*

"Check the local minor league baseball team schedule, he's their pitcher." Holly returned the paper to Edie when she was done writing.

"Anything else you can tell me about Nick?" Edie hoped Holly wouldn't take it as an invitation to discuss Nick Klein's sexual performance.

"No."

"Holly, where were you the night of Nick's death?"

Holly looked a little taken aback at the question. "Eating pizza."

"Can anyone confirm that?"

"Yes, everyone who was there."

"Can you be more specific as to the time and place?"

"I'll have to get back to you on that, after I've checked my credit card slips."

"Thank you, that would be wonderful. If you think of anything else, please call me. Here's my card."

Edie escorted Holly to the front door. She wanted to keep the other deputies safe. Edie watched Holly get into the elevator, then step out again.

"I forgot, I've been hearing rumors that Nicky was having an affair."

"Do you know who?"

"Nobody's been able to find out." Holly got back in the elevator. Edie and Holly stared at each other until the doors closed.

On returning to the interview room, Edie wanted a shower. The shit in this case was getting deeper.

The next time Edie looked at a clock, it was past time to pick up Hillary. She made a quick call to Aunt Jill to apologize.

"Don't worry, sweetie, I'm at your house. Thought I'd spend the night out here in the boonies. I've invited Hank to supper. We'll wait to eat until you get here. Bye."

Some days things work out. Today wasn't one of them, thought Edie.

TWENTY-TWO

THAT NIGHT EDIE walked into a cozy scene at home: the woodstove was throwing heat, Aunt Jill was in the kitchen putting food into serving dishes, Phil was sipping a brandy old-fashioned sweet, Hank Erb was picking Hillary's bottle off the floor—Hillary's newest sucker in her game of pick up my bottle. Edie stood in the doorway for a moment, unacknowledged by anyone, and thought about how easy it would be to slip into this tranquil domestic scene and leave the dirt of police work forever. But then she wondered who would step up to do that work. She glanced at Aunt Jill, who was beaming at Hank. It was a smile once reserved just for her, another reason not to quit the force—she needed to find out about Hank Erb. What could Aunt Jill really know about him?

Phil was the first to see Edie in the doorway. "Hi, want a drink?"

"No, thanks, not tonight."

"How'd your day go?"

"You don't want to know."

"That bad?" said Hank Erb.

"Supper's almost ready, if you haven't washed up, do so now," instructed Aunt Jill.

Edie understood that her aunt was attempting to re-direct her. Edie acquiesced, she didn't want a fight to-night. When she returned, Phil was blowing on Hillary's food to cool it down, and the food was being set in front of her own plate. It was a good ending of the day, roast chicken, mashed potatoes, and green beans, a scene reminiscent of Norman Rockwell's illustrations, and she felt the stress of her day melt.

Phil, finished with cooling down Hillary's food, was talking about his day. "Edie, you're not the only one who had a bad day. When I got to the shop this morning the tires were slashed on two of my trucks. The cops can't find the punks doing this soon enough. Then I got a call from my insurance agent about what they'll cover to paint the bay doors."

"You reported the tire slashing, right?"

"Of course I did. To the sheriff and the insurance agent, but that didn't fix the tires. My drivers weren't happy, my customers weren't happy, set everything back hours."

"Anyone hurt?"

"Nope."

"Set up those cameras yet?"

"Nope. Might be able to get to it tomorrow."

"Ever consider a security company?" Hank asked.

"If this keeps up, I will."

"Why not check on a security company now?" Hank continued.

"I'm still in the start-up phase of my company, don't know if I can afford them."

Carole's advice to not quit her day job was spot on, thought Edie.

"More reason to get a security system, you got more to lose. I got one the first time punks tried to steal my fuel."

"When was that?" asked Edie. Here was a concrete place to start her investigation of Hank.

Hank dropped his fork on his plate, leaned back in his chair, "Haven't thought about that in years, guess I'd rather forget those times, but it was when my Emily was really sick."

"Who is Emily?" asked Edie. She kept her eyes on Hank. She knew if she looked at her aunt that there would be silent signals to stop the interrogation. Edie didn't want to stop.

"My late wife. A couple of local punks stole some of my gas, couldn't stop them, I was busy with Emily. Got a security system installed the next day. Felt better. I was so angry at the world then, didn't know what I would do if I caught those boys on a different night. Probably would have shot them."

"Did you report it?"

"Yeah, but nothing came of it."

"When was that?"

"Must've been twenty years ago."

"Any ideas who did it?"

"None. Most likely local boys, they're the only ones who'd know where the tanks were, and stupid enough to drive these backroads with little to no fuel in their car."

The rest of the table was as quiet as Hank, except for Hillary, who dropped her bottle. The sound of the bottle hitting the floor seemed to bring Hank back to the present; he picked the bottle off the floor, placed it on Hillary's tray. There was a twinkle in his eyes. Hillary's game was back on.

Dinner was over. Phil took Hillary to clean her up and get her ready for bed, and Hank followed them. Edie and Aunt Jill stared at each other across the table.

"I know you had a hard day and would like to un-wind, but I'd like your help with the dishes," said Aunt Jill.

"I'll put them in the washer." Damn, thought Edie, what is she going to yell at me now for? I'm a grown woman, not a kid. I don't have to take this in my own house. But Edie stayed and listened.

"No, I want you and me to talk. Do you want to wash or dry?"

"Do I have a choice?"

"Not anymore, you're drying."

Edie cleared the table of dishes, then carried them to the sink. Even though she was an adult, she was dreading this talk. In the past, this was where Aunt Jill talked and Edie listened to all the suggestions that Aunt Jill thought Edie needed to improve her life.

It was awfully quiet while Edie put the leftovers in the fridge.

"Hank's a good man," Aunt Jill led off, as she filled the sink with hot water and soap.

"How do you know?"

"'Cause I do. How'd you know that Phil was a good man?"

"Partly because I saw that mine was his first arrest."

"That only means that he was never caught before then. How did you know he was a good person?"

"There was something about him. I went out with him, watched him during those dates. Everything I could see told me he was a good person."

"Same here. Everything I've seen of Hank, he's a good man."

"But what do you know about men? When was the last time you were with one?"

"Little one," said Aunt Jill. Edie knew she was in trouble. "My mother kept close watch on your mother

115

and me, but I did manage to have a life before you entered the picture. Remember, I've never asked about what you and the boys in your life did. I expect the same courtesy. And . . . this may shock you, but I wasn't a nun while I was raising you. I want you to lay off on Hank."

"But what if—"

"Then I'll call you." Aunt Jill handed the last pan to Edie, pulled the drain plug, and then left the kitchen. Edie watched her go; she would keep her promise to Aunt Jill to leave Hank alone, until she had the time to delve into his background.

TWENTY-THREE

THE NEXT MORNING, Edie held her tongue when Aunt Jill walked in through her door to watch Hillary. A promise was a promise, and she was grateful that her aunt was in the neighborhood—it meant that Phil and Hillary could sleep in.

Deputy Johnson stopped at Edie's desk after report. "Anything new at Phil's?"

"I wanted to ask the same of you. Just heard about the tire slashing," said Edie.

"Could be spring fever like Phil thinks, or someone doesn't like him or one of the drivers. I showed the pictures to the Gangs people, they don't see any known gang signs. The lab's identified the paint, but that's no help. That paint is sold everywhere."

"You're sticking with the theory that a gang's doing this?"

"Can't dismiss it, it's one of the possibilities. Wish Phil would get a security system setup."

"He promised to do that today."

"I hope he follows through. You know, Edie, this is turning into one devil of a case." Johnson shifted from one foot to the other. "Edie, you'll call me if anything else happens, won't you?"

"That's Phil's job, not mine. I'm busy with this murder case, Ren." As Johnson walked away it occurred to Edie that he might know Hank Erb. ""Hey, Ren, I need to talk to you for a moment."

Johnson returned to Edie's desk. "What do you need?"

"Do you know a Henry Erb?"

"Sure, big-time farmer around Troutbeck, nice guy. Pulled me out of the ditch this past winter. Why?"

"He's dating my aunt."

"Want me to keep an eye on him?"

"No, it's alright, just checking up on him, but thanks for the offer." Edie watched Johnson walk away. Of course, she had lots of questions about Henry Erb, but so far everyone thought him a good guy. She thought of one more question and opened her mouth to call Johnson back, but it died on her tongue—there was the dead man walking into the office. But it couldn't be, she told herself, that body was at the mortuary being prepared for the funeral tomorrow. But it could be him. Edie saw Johnson direct Nick Klein's body double toward her.

"Detective Swift?" he asked, when he stood in front of her desk.

"Yes, that's me," she said, shaking hands with him. Nice warm handshake for a dead man, she thought. "And you are?"

"Chad Bahr, you asked me to come in."

Edie shook hands with Chad, "Nice to meet you. I'll grab a notepad, and then we can go to an interview room."

"Do I need a lawyer?"

"Did you do anything wrong?"

"No. But on TV everyone is always demanding a lawyer."

"Well . . . I'm just gathering information about Nick Klein, but if you think you need a lawyer . . ." Edie waited a few moments as Chad thought through his options.

"I guess I'll talk with you. But why does everyone demand a lawyer?"

"Got me." Edie led the way to an interview room, motioned for Chad to take a seat across the table from her. "Can I get you something? Coffee, pop, water . . . a donut?"

A snort escaped Chad. "No, thanks, I'm laying off donuts for a while—noticed the beginnings of a love handle a few weeks ago."

"They're one of the perks of getting old. If you want something to drink, tell me, okay?"

"Sure."

"Let's get this started. Again, thanks for coming in. I'm looking for background on Nicholas Klein. I hope you can give me some insight into his life."

Chad took a deep breath, "Nick and I are cousins . . . is that the right tense?"

"Don't know, I'm not an English teacher. But I know what you mean."

"Anyway, we're cousins. He was a few years younger than me. Jay, Nick's brother, and I are the same age. We were called the three musketeers."

"The three of you righting wrongs?"

"No, but we did create a few—at least that is what our parents told us. No, we were always together. Went through school together, lived together until Jay got married."

"Nick ever in trouble when he was young?"

"Only kid stuff, skipping school, underage drinking on someone's back forty. Nick was a good kid."

"Do you know of anyone who wanted to harm him?"

"Nah, he was great to hang out with. He'd drop anything to hang out with you. That didn't sit well with the girls he knew. A few were boiling mad at him."

"Who was that?"

"His old fiancée and his wife."

"Why were they upset?"

"Nick . . . Nick was a chick magnet. I don't know what it was that attracted girls to him. It couldn't have been his looks. He and I could've been twins, and the girls never flocked around me."

"So, what would have upset his fiancée and wife?"

"As I said, Nick was a chick magnet, even when he was married. Maybe that's why his first fiancée dumped him. As did that baseball player's wife. The only one who stayed with him was that bitchy wife of his."

"Why do you call her bitchy?"

"Because after Nick met her, he rarely did anything with me and Jay."

"Why do you think that was?"

"Obvious, she had him by the short hairs."

Edie reminded herself that she was on duty and that her job was to get answers, not to correct stupid ones. "What can you tell me about Nick's other girls?"

"The baseball player's wife who dumped Nick?"

"Did he have more?"

"Not that anyone told me about."

"Then, do you know the name of the baseball player's wife?"

"No, Holly didn't tell me. It's all supposed to be hush-hush because he plays for the Madison league."

"Who is Holly?" Edie waited as she watched Chad turned scarlet from his collar to the roots of his hair.

Chad looked down. "Holly Sundby, the girl Nick should'a married."

Edie took a shot in the dark. "How did you two hook up?"

"Who?" A pink flush spread over Chad's face.

"You and Holly."

"I think it was sometime in high school. The musketeers would hang out with her. We taught her how to shoot; her favorite pastime was taking out stop signs. She found me. I hadn't seen her since she dropped Nick. She kept coming to the pizza place I manage. I got the idea she wanted more than pizza from me."

"How long have you and Holly been together?"

"A few months, but I'm going to dump her. I owe that to Nick."

"Who else did Nick hang out with?"

"There was Tom Brown, but he's been holed up since his wife died."

"How long has that been?"

"Ten, eleven years, maybe twelve years now. Didn't realize it was that long ago, seems like it happened yesterday."

"That's a long time to be holed up."

"Yeah, but how do get over having your wife murdered? Some people still think he murdered her."

"Did he?"

"No, he loved her. Wish you guys would put more effort into finding Mamie Robin's killer."

"Murder investigations are never really closed."

"Yeah, I know, they're called cold cases."

"Yes, they are. What was Mamie Robin's full name?"

"Mamie Robin Brown."

"What was her maiden name?" Edie did a silent shudder, family names, family names—maiden names should have been dropped from everyone's vocabulary at least two centuries ago.

"I think it was Neu-something. Yeah, that was it . . . Mamie Robin Neuport Brown. Granddaughter to the ol' man Acker who lives in Troutbeck.

"Harold Acker from Troutbeck?"

"Yeah. He's the one. Did you know he used to be a bouncer at the strip joint in Lower Bottom? Who does he think he is making the rest of us feel guilty about going to those strip clubs?"

Keep your mouth shut and you can learn a lot of things, thought Edie. "Anything else you can tell me about Nick? Any other friends I should talk with?"

"There's another high school friend we'd hang out with, Lee Mitchell."

"How can I get in touch with Lee Mitchell?" Edie knew this, but there was no reason for Chad to know that.

"Difficult this time of year, unless he got his limit."

"What does that mean?" Edie saw the look on Chad's face that she'd seen on many men's faces: *what can you expect from a woman?* She let the challenge pass.

"Lee loves hunting, he'll shoot anything. If there's a season for hunting it, he's got a permit."

"Where does Lee Mitchell live?"

"Out near Troutbeck, I can e-mail you his address."

"Thank you," said Edie, handing Chad her business card. "Anything else you can tell me about Nicholas Klein?"

"No."

"If you remember anything, call me, you've got my card." Edie escorted Chad to the elevator.

"This is going to make a great story, me coming into the sheriff's office," said Chad as they waited for the elevator.

"Don't embellish it too much, okay?'

"That would take all the fun out of it," Chad said, getting into the elevator.

"One more thing, Chad, what were you doing the night of Nick's death?"

"Making pizza for Holly Sundby," said Chad, his face turning scarlet.

"And—"

"Other stuff."

"For how long?"

"All night."

Edie wondered how in the world Chad's face could turn a deeper red, but it did.

The doors closed. Edie watched until the elevator lights indicated that it had stopped at the first floor. Thinking over the case, she wondered if people ever left their high school feuds behind when they graduated, or maybe some people graduated high school, but never left the building. She walked back to her desk to write up a report on her interview with Chad Bahr when Mamie Robin Neuport Brown's name popped into her thoughts; she should pull that case file.

TWENTY-FOUR

EDIE SCRATCHED OUT her latest draft of her interview with Chad Bahr; it was hard to write a politically correct report when what she really wanted to describe was one more asshole stuck in adolescence. She looked over at Gracie's office, the door was open and she was in. Edie gathered all the drafts of the report, stuffed them into the shredder, and then went to see Gracie.

She waited in the doorway for Gracie to acknowledge her knock.

It took a moment for Gracie to look up. "What can I do for you Detective?"

"I need to bounce some ideas off someone."

"And you chose me. Why not the other detectives?

"They looked busy."

Gracie laid down her pen, then leaned back in her chair, "Come on in and have a seat." Edie walked into the office and settled into the chair opposite Gracie. "How's your case going?"

"I'm having problems writing the report on my last interview. The interviews I've had to date make my dysfunctional family look normal."

"Stick with the facts, easiest things to remember in court, just the facts. Remember no one is at their best behavior when a family member's been murdered."

"I'd think they could at least stop calling the widow a bitch. And the cousin at least has the decency to claim he's going to stop screwing the dead man's first fiancée. So far, the dead man seems to have had a stack of affairs, and the men on the sidelines watching were cheering him on. The list of suspects is growing, and it's mostly women . . . I am so eager to interview the next woman. Tell me, why do women have affairs with married men?"

"Haven't figured that one out. Put a wedding ring on a man's finger and it seems that women start lining up to pull it off. Happened to me. That floozy started to flaunt her stuff in front of my Martin and he started drooling. I set them both right. It never happened again."

"Am I naïve to think there's ever been such a thing as sisterhood? Aren't we supposed to stick together?"

"Some never got the message. But what does this have to do with your case?"

"It seems that musical beds were played, and jealousy has a way of clogging up the brain."

"You think this case is about jealousy."

"Maybe, but I don't know whose. I'll tell you what I've got on the case: the wife of the dead man, who married him when he was on the rebound, and knew about a few of his affairs; an ex-fiancée of the dead man who may have been having second thoughts and bedded down with him a number of times after his marriage, and is now doing the same with his look-alike cousin; a brother who's already convicted the widow of murder. And the next interview is with a woman who had an affair with the dead man, again, while the guy was married."

"Throw sex into the mix, anything is likely to happen. Anything else?'

"How long have you been on the force?"

"I meant about the cemetery case. I'll have to call HR on the exact date, but it's been around sixteen years. Why?"

"So, it was a few years before we met."

"Yeah, I was still on patrol at that time. Why do you ask?"

"Was hoping you'd remember a murder of ten, maybe twelve years ago, a Mamie Robin Neuport Brown?"

"Give me a moment." Gracie leaned back in her chair, closed her eyes.

Edie waited. If Gracie had worked the case, it might take a long time to sift through the years and locate those memories. Edie remembered vividly each murder case she had been on, and Gracie had been on the force a long time.

"Got it, I was on that case," said Gracie. "I'm surprised you don't remember it—young girl, Sun Prairie area, husband came home from work to find her murdered. Cleared him of the murder, but I suppose suspicions linger around him still. Hard to shake those malicious whispers in a cold case. I remember every one of my cases that involved a murder. For me, it's those cases that were never solved that seem to stick out the most in my memory. Surprised you don't remember it, big news story at the time. Were you on the force then? Maybe you were on jail rotation at the time. Why do you ask?"

"Her name popped up in an interview today."

Gracie's eyes seemed to bore into Edie. "I thought I was handing you a straightforward murder case. I was wrong. How did I forget that you and trouble always collide? You pulling the Brown case file?"

"Of course."

TWENTY-FIVE

IT WAS NIGHT and the morning's interview with Chad Bahr was still bugging Edie, she couldn't find the pattern to Nick Klein's murder and Chad's interview had jumbled it more. Something was needed to clear her brain. She pulled on her running gear.

When Edie entered the living room, Phil looked up from the truck manual he was studying. "Jogging this late?"

"Gotta clear my mind. Hillary's asleep."

"How long are you going to be gone?"

"Don't know."

"It's a clear night, it'll get cold while you're out, better wear your winter-weight running jacket."

Edie pulled the jacket from the closet.

"Got your cell?"

"Yes. I don't leave home without it." Enough of this questioning, Edie wanted to scream; I've been in control of my own life for a long time now. Leave me alone, I can handle this.

"Good. I got you a headlamp for when you jog at night. I'll get it." Phil went into the laundry room. Edie heard drawers opening and doors slammed. He returned triumphantly with the headlamp, slipped it on Edie's head, then adjusted it. She felt like a kid.

"Got your gun?"

"I'm off duty. The gun is under lock and key in the closet. I don't need it. Now do you want me to take the kitchen sink too?"

"If it keeps you safe, yes."

"I'll be fine," Edie said, closing the door behind her. Edie took a deep breath, walked into the night and off the step. *Do something, she told herself, anything before the fear comes, before I can't move, before I turn back.* She started to jog.

Edie was in the shadow of the vacant corner store when she heard footsteps. She thrust her elbow back, and then swung around to face whoever was behind her.

"Matilda!" Edie looked around. *Did someone send her to run with me?* Someone was always appearing at her side during the winter when she went out. And now they were sending kids. Enough already, Edie wanted to shout.

"Yes," Matilda was able to squeak out from a doubled-over position.

"Did I hurt you?"

"I don't think so," Matilda said, beginning to stand up. "Why did you do that?"

"Reflex action. Why didn't you announce yourself? And never do that again."

"Didn't think I had to, Mrs. Best."

"My name is Edie Swift. I'm not married."

"Really? You are not married and you have a baby! What does Troutbeck think of that?"

"It's not Troutbeck's concern."

"Do you know Troutbeck? Of course it is."

Edie thought it was none of Matilda VandenHuevel's business either. "What are you doing out this late on a school night?" Edie watched as Matilda struggled to find an answer. "Do your parents know you are out?"

"No, they're sleeping in front of the TV."

Edie studied the girl for a moment. "So, what do you want from me, Matilda?"

"To talk with you."

Edie saw Matilda's shoulders relax. "Can you talk and run at the same time?"

"I'm not much of a runner, can we walk?"

"Not my favorite speed, but okay." Edie started out fast, and then looked down at the girl trying to keep pace with her; she adjusted her stride so Matilda might keep up with her.

"What was that you were humming back there?" Matilda asked.

"Just humming. Was it recognizable?"

"No. You were doing it last week, too. Why do you hum when you run?"

If anyone else asked that question, Edie would have peppered the person with expletives for invading her privacy. Matilda's questions jettisoned her back to the time when she stood on the brink of adulthood and was seeking answers. No one replied. Edie remembered thinking that adults were the strangest, disconnected weirdos in the world.

Now here at her side was a young woman seeking answers. Edie answered the question with the same bluntness Matilda had used. "I was scared."

"You scared? I didn't know cops get scared."

"We do. We get past it because that's what we promised to do. And if we can't, we quit. Being a cop is like being IT in tag all the time—you've signed on to be the one to do something, and you gotta do it."

Matilda was quiet for a moment. "Do you like your job?"

"I do. I think being a cop and Hillary's mom are the bestest jobs in the world."

"Why'd you become a cop?"

"A friend got hurt, some cops helped her, and I wanted to be able to do that for others who found themselves in bad situations."

"What do you know about boys?"

"Not much. The older I get, the less I know. To adapt a Churchill quote: Boys are a riddle wrapped in a mystery inside an enigma. But, still, they're kinda nice to have around. Have you asked your mom these questions, or your girlfriends?"

"Yeah, but they don't know either." Matilda didn't say anything for a moment. "How do you know if a guy likes you?"

"Depends on the age. Usually they do nice things for you. Why?"

"There's this one . . . um . . . boy that my . . . um, my friend says looks at her weird."

"Good weird or bad weird?"

"I don't know. I've never seen the weird look, I've only heard about it."

"I used to tell my friends to go with your guts. If it tells you to leave, get the hell out of there—fast."

"What does that mean?"

"Gut feeling is when you can't put two and two together, but you know something isn't right. Don't ever overrule that feeling."

There was silence between the two women. Edie sensed that there was something more that Matilda wanted to ask. She knew to wait, not to fill the void.

"Mom said you need a babysitter."

"I'm looking for one. Are you offering your services?"

"I am, just for an hour or two, occasionally. Do you need one Saturday?"

"Why Saturday?"

"I'm free then."

"I'll talk with Phil about his schedule, then call your mother if we need you."

"No, call me, then I'll tell her."

"That's fine, but I need a call from her. I want to know that it is okay."

"Okay." Matilda wasn't finished. "Could I bring my cousin? She just got her driver's license and sometimes she just drives up here without telling us. She might come up this weekend."

"That changes things. I really need to talk with your mother before Saturday. Can you vouch for your cousin?"

"She babysits at home all the time. Kids love her."

"Okay, I'll wait to hear from your mother before making this final." Edie stopped in front of Matilda's house. "I think this is your place. When you get inside, I want you to wave to me." Edie watched as Matilda ran to the back of her house. A few seconds later Matilda was waving from the front window. Edie waved back, then jogged home certain that Matilda wanted to talk about something more than babysitting. She hoped that Matilda would talk about what was bugging her in her own good time.

TWENTY-SIX

"DID I TELL you that I was going to the Klein visitation tonight?" Edie shouted, stuffing more diapers into the bulging diaper bag.

"Four, five . . . no, six times," Phil said, walking into Hillary's room half-shaved.

"Do you want to come with me?"

"No."

"Why not be blunt about it?"

"I live with a cop, I gotta tell the truth. If I don't, she'll beat it outta me."

"In your wildest dreams."

"No, my wildest dreams are sweeter than that," Phil said, falling onto the bed with Edie in his arms.

"Wasn't last night enough?"

"Once is never enough."

"It will have to be. I've got an interview," Edie said, flipping Phil onto his back. "And Hillary is watching."

Phil looked across the room at their daughter standing in her crib and clapping. "Hi, sweetie, I forgot you were there. Did you know that you are in demand today? First you go by Aunt Jill, and then you and I are going to Nana's."

"Are you eating at your mother's?"

"Do you need to ask? She'll start stuffing me when I walk in. Umm . . . since you're busy tonight, thought Hillary and I would spend the night there."

"Thought you might, it makes my weekend manageable. I've packed plenty of diapers and clothes for Hillary. That should pass Lorraine's inspection. You need to pack for yourself. Say hi for me."

"A thaw? You two might actually talk!"

"Hardly, negotiations haven't gone that far. Just say hi. I just thought of it, you never say anything about Lorraine insisting we get married. When was the last time your mother asked about us getting married?"

"I don't remember," Phil said, lifting Hillary out of her crib.

"You are lying, but I don't have time to explain cultural shifts to you or your mother. I gotta run," said Edie, kissing them both. "Could you be home early on Saturday? I'm arranging for Matilda to meet Hillary."

"We don't need another sitter."

"I think we do, gotta run. Bye."

Edie watched the clock. Ashley Zielinski was late. No sense starting a new project, Zielinski would probably interrupt it.

Twenty minutes past the scheduled time Edie threw in the towel. She pulled out the Klein file to review. Absorbed in the case notes, she didn't look up until someone cleared their throat. A young, leggy brunette stood in front of Edie's desk.

"Hi, I'm Ashley Zielinski. Sorry I'm late."

"I'm Detective Swift—"

"I know, a clerk pointed you out."

Edie extended her hand; Ashley looked at it for a moment, and then extended her hand. For Edie, it barely

133

counted as a handshake. Zielinski's hand was there and pulled back in a second. "Thanks for coming in, we'll use one of the interview rooms." Edie picked up a notebook and led the way to the back. "Can I get you something to drink, Mrs. Zielinski?"

"No thanks, I'm meeting someone for coffee after I'm finished here," she said as she settled into a chair. "And, please, call me Ashley."

Edie settled into the chair opposite Ashley, opened the notebook, and squiggled a few circles to make sure that the pen was working. "Again, Ashley, thank you for coming in. The purpose of this interview is to get some background information on Nicholas Klein."

"I thought Holly gave you everything."

"Holly who?"

"My good friend Holly Sundby. She told me all about you."

"Good to know. How do you know Holly Sundby?"

"We're shopping and shooting buddies. She's got good clothes taste and can she shoot. With her accuracy, she should be on some type of national team, maybe the Olympics."

"I'll make a note of that. For now, I'm interested in hearing what you can tell me about Nick Klein."

"Good-looking. Good in bed. Sweet."

"Anything else you can tell me?"

"Don't know if I can, I only knew him for a few months. And we didn't spend that time discussing the world's problems. Nor our own, for that matter. Holly introduced us, said she was going to dump him, again, and wondered if I wanted him."

"What happened that you knew him for only a few months?"

"His wife found out."

"Who ended the relationship, you or Nick?"

"Nick did. I just don't understand what our fling had to do with his marriage. I'm married, he's married . . . what's the big deal?"

Edie wondered why she was offended by that statement: she must be getting old, or maybe she was absorbing Troutbeck morals by osmosis, maybe it was having a baby, or did she have her head screwed on right. "Do you know—?"

"You cops are so cliché. I've already told you Nick was a sweet guy, do anything for you at the drop of a hat. Who'd want to hurt him?"

The list of suspects is growing. "Did your husband know about your affair with Nick?"

"Don't be silly, of course he did. He has his flings. I have mine. They don't interfere with our marriage and, no, we don't discuss them."

Edie searched for the word that Aunt Jill used to describe those marriages—open. Open. Aunt Jill always followed it with 'why get married at all?' "Is there anything else you can think of about Nick?"

"Have you thought that Nick's wife might have killed him?"

"Why do you say that?"

"I'm sure she was angry about Nick and me, made him stop seeing me. I guess she was jealous, an acceptable reason for killing someone. I just don't understand women like her, a little something on the side spices up a marriage."

"Can you tell me where you were the night Nick was murdered?"

"Chicago. Enjoying a weekend with my husband. In a few more weeks, I won't be able to see him much as, his baseball season will be in full swing."

And so will your season, thought Edie.

Edie returned to her desk after seeing Ashley Zielinski to the elevator. "If only, if only," she murmured.

"If only, what?" Gracie asked, stopping at Edie's desk.

"If only that woman charged for her time, I could charge her with prostitution."

"Case getting to you? I can assign someone to assist."

"I can handle the case, it's the extraneous slime that's getting hard to handle. How do you raise your kids in times like these?"

"Do you want a philosophical discussion on today's mores, or practical solutions?"

"Practical solutions."

"Wrap them in love, keep them busy, and a good eye on them."

"And the boys?"

"They're scared of me, I'm a lieutenant with the sheriff's office. When was the last time you were at the firing range?"

"Last fall."

"Then you and I are going on Sunday."

"Isn't that your family day?"

"It is. I'm talking about going to the range early."

"That's my day to sleep in."

"Sleep some other time. See you Sunday morning at the range. Eight a.m."

Edie watched her boss walk away. Maybe someday she'd figure out how to tell her boss and friend to take a long walk off a short pier.

TWENTY-SEVEN

AT NOON EDIE stood on the Capitol Square looking down State Street. The sidewalks were filled with people the whole mile from the Capitol to Bascom Hill. She hadn't been on the street since last fall, and she didn't need to be there today. Plenty of good restaurants around the Capitol Square to eat. She turned away from State Street to walk to her favorite Irish pub and there, two feet away, was Mark Uselman, friend and reporter, staring at her.

"Why didn't you say hi?" Edie asked.

"Did that, didn't get a response from you. I learned my lesson months ago not to get too close to you when you're unaware. Besides, it looked like you might be on a case."

"I was only wondering where I should eat."

"Me, too. I'm thinking that the art museum would be great, but it's only open for dinner."

"Want to join me at the Clochen Dichter?"

"Drinking lunch today?"

"Can't, I'm on duty."

"Doesn't mean I can't lift a few."

"On your own tab."

Winds blowing across the stretches of ice still on Lake Mendota and swirling around the square had Edie and Mark retreating into their jackets, and made talk impossible during their walk to the Clochen Dichter.

The pub was as Edie remembered: warm, dark, friendly. The first floor was swarming with the lunch crowd from the Capitol, as usual—normally it was fun to listen in on the gossip from legislative staff members about the machinations of politicians that they worked for, but Edie and Mark were looking for something quieter, a place for them to talk without being overheard.

As they followed the waitress to a window seat, a voice demanding the check caught Edie's attention. She looked to her left; there sat Madonna Theis. Hers was a hard voice to forget. Edie and Madonna stared at each other, unable to move, caught in a magnetic force. Mark nudged Edie forward, breaking the bond, but not before Edie looked right, toward Madonna's companion, Ashley Zielinski. It felt natural to see the two women together. Mark kept nudging Edie past the booth toward the waitress.

"I'm thirsty, let's find a seat," said Mark. He turned to the waitress, "We'd like something more private."

The waitress gave them an understanding look and led them to the last booth, the one near the kitchen where only the staff might hear them. Edie sat so she could face the whole room. Uselman sat opposite her.

"Who's the bottle blonde?" Uselman asked.

"Didn't see anyone," Edie said, watching the lunch crowd leave the Clochen Dichter for the Capitol.

"Looked like you did. And that you know both those women. Who are they? Come on, tell me, friend to friend."

"Are you going to use it in a story?"

"No, I swear on my mother's grave."

"Your mother's alive."

"Okay. I promise that I'm not using it in a story, or . . . or I'll buy supper for you and Phil." Mark crossed his heart.

"With drinks?"

"With drinks," Mark spit out.

Edie knew Mark was telling the truth. He only bought drinks on someone else's expense account. "Off the record, one is the mother of the devil's spawn."

"Do they have names?"

"That would be Erik Theis' mother—Madonna."

"Hmmmm, too rich for my pocketbook."

"What's the hmmm for?"

"Just one of those serendipitous moments."

"What two and two are you putting together?"

"Money and politics and rumors floating around of another John Doe investigation."

"Another one? How many does that make?"

"Three. The Theis have money, right?"

"Their house screams money. But they could be up to their eyeballs in debt, you never know."

"And the Theis have friends in high places, right?"

"So they claim."

"Then you put two and two together."

"Damn," said Edie, hitting the table with her fist. "What's happened to Wisconsin? We were once known for having good government."

"And now we're competing with Illinois about who's going to have the most politicians in the big house."

"Couldn't we keep our rivalry on the football field?"

Someone stopped at their booth. "Ms. Swift, how nice to see you out and about." Edie recognized the suave voice of Jake Thomas. She and Uselman stopped talking and looked up at the intruder. "And Mr. Uselman, I am so pleased to finally meet you. I enjoy reading your work. That was a wonderful column of yours in the

Sunday paper. Maybe you and I can work together sometime. I could use someone to polish my prose. I'd love to stop and chat more, but my lunch companions are waiting. May I suggest you order the shepherd's pie today? It is delicious."

Edie and Mark watched him join Madonna Theis and Ashley Zielinski, then link arms with each woman as they exited the pub.

"Who is that?" asked Mark.

"Jake Thomas. We should have taken the window seat. I could've seen where they were going."

"Never heard of him. What does he do?"

"I've been told independent IT work."

"Thought I caught a whiff of money."

"Hmmm," said Edie.

"Now it's my turn. What's the hmmming about?"

"I never connected the two."

"What two?"

"Thomas and the Theises. Saw them at the Drunken Duck last fall. Lots of reasons people are in the same bar together, isn't there? Sometimes it's planned, sometimes not. What were we talking about?"

"Money."

"What will that get you?"

"Nice home, clothes, vacations, food, wine, and for me, some really good-looking women. Do you need anything else beyond that? Not me. Hey, come on tell me, who's the brunette who gave me the once over?"

"A baseball player's wife."

"Got her number?"

"No."

"Know where I can find her?"

"For work or pleasure?"

"Haven't decided."

"I'm not pimping for you."

"Wasn't going to charge her anything."

"You can find her at the ball park, watching her husband pitch."

"I love baseball."

Edie doubted that. "When was the last time you played the game?"

"High school gym class."

"When was the last time you watched a game?"

"Last fall. Last game of the World Series."

"Sure you did. But, if your interest in the sport deepens, I'm never a topic of conversation. Got that?"

"You never are."

"Keep it that way."

Edie and Mark put their conversation on hold while the waitress took their order. Edie ordered shepherd's pie; Mark ordered a pint of Spotted Cow and a burger.

"You could've ordered that anywhere," said Edie.

"The burgers are good here. It was your choice to eat here. And you ordered the shepherd's pie, his suggestion."

"I've seen his house, he's got good taste."

"Socializing with the upper crust; are you getting too rich for my blood?"

"Not on my salary."

The two old friends had used up all the small talk they could think of.

Edie broached the unspoken topic. "It was the first time looking at State Street since last year. Nearly peed my pants."

Mark wasn't ready for that discussion. He tried to steer their conversation away from that topic. "How's the investigation?"

"Which one?"

"You got more than one murder going on? I'll take the body in the cemetery one."

141

"Slow."

"What you finding?"

"Dysfunctional families."

"Aren't we all?"

"How are the trials going?"

"Haven't started. The Theis kid got an expensive lawyer, and rumor has it that a few strings have been pulled."

"Where'd the rumor start?"

"Leigh Stone."

"Any truth to it?"

"Don't know, but she might have something, she's been moving up in the network. Any higher she'll be out of this market."

"Not a loss."

"What has she done to you . . . lately?" Mark asked, as their food was being served.

Edie concentrated on the food as Mark filled her in on the last six months.

After lunch, Edie walked to the parking ramp alone. Every muscle in her body was tense. Her gut was telling her something. She looked around. No one in sight. She unzipped her winter coat, opened her suit coat wider, and felt for her gun. It was still in its holster.

She was a few feet from her car when she heard it, a car minus a muffler making its way through the parking ramp. She pushed the unlock button on the car key, and in a few steps was in her car with the doors locked, and her gun was in her hand. She put her head on the steering wheel and cried. "Get hold of yourself Edie. If you can't, they win. That means they control you for the rest of your life. Time to choose, Edie. It's you or them." Edie took three deep breaths, letting each out slowly. The shudder that followed released some of her tension. She put her gun back in its holster. Wiped the tears from her face. Felt through her coat pocket for the piece of paper that Gracie had handed to her on Monday. She stared at it for a few moments, found her cell, then punched in the number that was on the paper and left a message. "Hi, this is Edie Swift, I'd like to talk with someone from the peer support group. I can be reached at this number."

TWENTY-EIGHT

EDIE HAD TOLD Carole the plan for the Friday night funeral visitation for Nicholas Klein many times. They—her, Carole, and Sera—were to be early to the funeral home so Edie could pay her condolences to Mariah Collins, the grieving widow, then sit discreetly in a corner to monitor the mourners as they passed through the receiving line. That Carole and Sera would provide a cover story for her while she, Edie, observed the people coming and going. Each time, Carole said yes, she understood the plan. But here Edie was sitting on her front step, twiddling her thumbs, waiting for Carole to show up. She should have stuck to her original plan of meeting Carole and Sera at the funeral home.

When Carole did show up she explained that Ray had to be given last-minute instructions, again, on how to reheat his dinner. Then Sera, after looking through her purse, said she needed to stop at an ATM to get cash for the memorial envelope. Edie felt she was being sucked deeper into Troutbeck's culture. Was there time to save herself and Hillary?

With ten cars in the funeral home's parking lot when they drove in, Edie wondered how many people had already come and left, and what countless opportunities were lost of seeing the external dynamics of Nick Klein's life. What opportunities had she missed to narrow or expand her list of possible murderers? Then thoughts of Holly Sundby popped into her head. Would she be there? That would provide one more gossip thread for Troutbeck to pick over during the coming weeks . . . maybe months. Of course, Chad Bahr would be there. What about Ashley Zielinski? Edie started to giggle over the possibilities of unplanned encounters. She couldn't help herself. This evening had the makings of a great soap opera. Edie told herself to suck it up. She wasn't in control of the universe and this evening was a funeral, not a carnival sideshow. Tonight she wanted people to see her as being neighborly, not doing her detective work.

Edie need not have worried, the list of people signing the condolence book was as short as the line of people offering Mariah condolences. And the people who had signed the guest book were shorter than that. Mariah thanked Edie, Carole, and Sera for coming, and while Carole and Sera lingered to tell stories of Nick when he was young, Edie looked over the photo display of Nick's life.

It was easy to pick out the three musketeers—Nick, Jay, and Chad. They seemed to have gone everywhere together, and even in large group pictures they weren't separated: Jay in the middle with his arms around Nick and Chad, and another young boy who stood near them. Edie looked closer at the group pictures to see if she could identify anyone. Holly, always next to another young girl, beamed at the camera. A young man stood behind Holly, staring with hunger at the girl next to her. There was one of Mariah and Nick on their wedding day, radiant. Edie wondered how long it had taken Mariah to lose that glow. Children's laughter flowed into the viewing room. Edie turned toward the sound. How odd to hear sounds of joy during this time of sorrow. In the back room, she saw Jay playing with children and adults eating nearby. Then a pregnant woman closed the door when she saw Edie staring. Edie wanted to tell the woman that her move was futile; a closed door couldn't keep life at bay.

Edie looked around the room for a suitable corner to watch the passing parade from, one that would give her an expansive view of the spaces used for Nicholas Klein's visitation. She secured the corner and arranged three chairs. When Carole and Sera finally joined Edie, they scooted their chairs closer, leaned in, and began their assessment of the gathering.

"Looks as if it's going to be a short night," Carole said.

"It's early, most people will come after work," Sera said.

"Recognize anyone?" Edie asked.

"Not yet," Carole and Sera said in unison.

"Haven't seen any of Nick's family. I think the people out here are most likely to belong to Mariah," Sera said.

"How many siblings did Nick have?" Edie asked.

"The only ones I know of are Jay and Erica," Carole said.

"You think there's more?" Edie asked.

"You never know, apples don't fall far from the tree," Sera said.

"Are you hinting at something?" Edie asked.

"Well, Jay and Nick have to take after someone," Sera said.

"Are you saying things aren't kosher in the Klein family?"

"In my mother's day, it was called sowing your wild oats," Sera said.

"I'm guessing that euphemism for sleeping around was used for men only. Call it what it is—whoring," Carole said.

"No, that's what they called the girls who did the same thing—whores," Sera said.

"And back then, what did they say about the boys?" Carole asked.

"Boys will be boys," Sera replied.

"That double standard should be deep-sixed. Call them both whores," Carole said.

"You're taking a wide view," Sera said.

"If the name fits the goose, it should fit the gander," Carole said.

"Who's the young woman that just came in?" Edie asked.

Carole and Sera looked her over, shrugged their shoulders, and leaned toward Edie. The consensus was that she looked kind of like Mariah, probably a cousin.

"I'm glad they chose a closed coffin," Sera said.

"I heard they had to, lots of trauma to the head. Isn't that right, Edie?" Carole asked.

"You know I can't comment on an ongoing investigation," Edie said.

"More like you won't," Carole said.

"It saves my friends from being deposed before trials," Edie said.

"Surprised he's not being cremated," Sera said.

"Rumor is that there was a huge argument about that between Nick's family and Mariah. That Mariah gave in and is letting him be buried here," Carole said.

"Carole, why am I here? I could have come to your salon and learned all this, and more besides," Edie said. "Who's the man that came in?"

"Don't know, looks familiar, though," Carole said.

Sera gasped. "That's Tom Brown. My God, has he aged."

"That's him! I thought he left the area," Carole said.

"Who is Tom Brown?" Edie asked. Of course, she knew, but she wasn't going to jeopardize learning more about her case by name-dropping with her neighbors.

"Thought you knew about him. It was big news when it happened," Sera said.

"One of the scariest days of my life," Carole said. "I woke up that morning to sirens descending on Troutbeck, just like last Friday."

"It was terrible. No one went out after dark for a long time," Sera said.

"What happened?" Edie asked.

"Tom Brown's wife, Mamie Robin, was murdered," Sera said.

"She was Harold Acker's granddaughter," Carole said.

"Did they ever catch who did it?" Edie asked.

"No, it was assumed that Tom Brown did it, but that couldn't be proved. Maybe you can look into it," Sera said.

"Maybe, but I have to finish this one first, before tackling a cold case."

The trio quieted down to watch as Tom Brown said a few words to Mariah, hugged her, lingered at Nick's coffin with his head down, then lightly swept his hand over the coffin before moving on to the photo display of Nick Klein's life. Carole and Sera didn't know the next couple who entered the room. A woman who looked like Mariah went through the line then went to the back room; they guessed her to be Mariah's sister. Then Jay and his sister, Erica, came out of the back room and took their places in the receiving line. Moments later, a wave of Troutbeck residents entered the funeral home. Edie was surprised she knew so many. They, in turn, were surprised to see her. But they satisfied their curiosity by greeting the trio and being informed by Sera that Edie was being a very good neighbor by accompanying her to the funeral home.

"Oh, look who walked in. This is going to be good," whispered Carole. "Didn't know if she would show up."

"Who?" asked Edie, still concentrating on the line of people offering their condolences to Nick's family.

"Holly Sundby," Carole and Sera said in unison.

"Nick Klein's first fiancée," Sera informed Edie.

Edie noticed the room had become quiet. Anyone who knew anything seemed to be watching Holly Sundby. What would she do?

Edie watched as Holly Sundby made her entrance. She was dressed in a figure-revealing black dress, black stilettos, her single diamond solitaire pendant visible, her blonde hair cascading down her back, and had reddened eyes. She had come alone. Edie looked around for Chad Bahr. She saw him creep into the back room and softly close the door. She turned back to watch as Holly made her way through the receiving line. The Klein clan embraced her, each clinging to her, maybe a little too long, then passing her on to the next family member. Until, finally the old fiancée and the widow were face to face. Mariah did not extend her hand to her late husband's ex-fiancée and seemed to take a step away from Holly. Holly's long curls bounced as she tossed her head, and she moved on to briefly offer her condolences to the rest of the Collins family. Then she stood at the coffin with her hand resting on it.

"No love lost there," whispered Carole.

"Why not?" asked Edie, hoping to hear more of the gossip surrounding Nick Klein.

"One more soap opera. Rumor has it that Holly and Nick had an affair. She should have just married him," said Carole.

"I doubt that marriage would have lasted long," said Sera.

"Why not?" asked Edie.

"Those Kleins don't like women who have brains," said Sera.

"I used to think that nothing happened in Troutbeck," said Edie.

"Nothing much does," said Sera.

They focused their attention back on Holly, who kissed the closed coffin, then moved on to the photo display, where she stood next to Tom Brown and put her arm around him.

Edie looked around the room. While Tom Brown and Holly Sundby seemed to be rooted in front of the photo display, the crowd was thinning, the receiving line was getting restless, and it was time to go home. But Carole and Sera saw one more person they simply had to talk to.

Edie gathered up the coats and followed them. She handed each woman her coat, then saw that Sera had stopped talking. Edie followed Sera's gaze to a woman who had entered the viewing room. The woman was about five-foot-four, but seemed shorter. Her hair was salt and pepper, and she wore a black coat, black pants. She could have been mistaken for a shadow, thought Edie.

"This is too sad," said Sera. "She didn't have to come."

"Who?" asked Edie.

"Sandy Neuport, Harold Acker's daughter, mother to Mamie Robin," said Sera. "Excuse me, I have to talk with her. We can leave after that."

Edie and Carole watched as Sera spent a few moments talking with Sandy Neuport.

"Tonight's going to make some great talk next week at the salon. The current town gossip is getting kind of stale," said Carole.

"You'll tell me what's said, won't you?" asked Edie.

"Ooh, I get to be your handy crime-solving partner. Who am I Lois Lane, Kato, Robin—oh, that's a bad choice of names tonight," said Carole.

"You can choose your own alias, but for now, we'll keep your identity under wraps," said Edie. She watched as Sandy Neuport went through the receiving line, passed the coffin, and then stopped. In front of her was Tom Brown, still looking at the photo display. She turned away from him, and slipped as quickly and quietly out of the room as when she had entered it.

"This is just sad. I don't think Sandy and Tom have been in the same room since the funeral. Let's go," said Sera.

Chilled night air seeped into the room, Edie turned to see who had let it in—Crystal Mitchell. She and Edie exchanged nods. Edie watched as Crystal offered her condolences and then walked to the closed coffin. Mariah joined her, and the women draped their arms around each other, two statutes lost to the world.

"Let's stay for a few more minutes," said Edie.

Chill night air swept into the room once more. Everyone turned to see who the latecomer was. Mariah went back to the receiving line, and Crystal joined Holly Sundby at the photo display, sandwiching Tom Brown between them. Carole and Sera rejoined Edie.

"Who is that man who just came in?" asked Edie.

Carole and Sera turned to look.

"Lee Mitchell. Surprised he came to his friend's funeral instead of being out in some field. So he isn't totally selfish," said Carole.

"I've never heard you talk about a client like that," said Edie.

"He isn't a client."

"Time we left," said Sera.

"Let's not, this night is getting better and better. I didn't know funerals could be so entertaining," said Carole.

"I don't want to leave yet, either. I'd like to meet Lee Mitchell," said Edie. She observed Lee Mitchell as he spoke briefly with Mariah, walked quickly past his friend's coffin, and then joined the people at the photos. Tom Brown left. Lee hugged Holly. Crystal moved closer to her husband and placed her arm around him. He shrugged it off. She then rested a hand on his shoulder as they stood side by side viewing the pictures of better times, when they were all young together. Crystal leaned toward Lee, whispered something to him. Lee turned around and stared at Edie. Crystal took his hand and pulled him to Edie.

"Thanks for helping Crystal out the other day," said Lee.

"Nice to meet you, Mr. Mitchell. It was no problem, just helping out a neighbor. I was wondering if you had time to talk with me?" said Edie.

"About what?"

"Nick Klein."

Lee hung his head. "It's been a rough week. He was my friend and I've lost him. Didn't know it would be this rough."

"I'm sorry for your loss. I have heard that you were a close friend of Nick's. It would be helpful to hear more about him from you."

"He was a good friend. Hope you get the bastard who did this."

"Maybe with your insight we can. I could come by your workplace."

"My boss is letting me work odd hours this week, whenever I feel up to it. He understands what I'm going through, so he doesn't like me being interrupted. Why don't you call me next week? Maybe I'll be better by then. Nice meeting you, Mrs. Best. Hi, Sera, Carole." Lee put his hand on Crystal's back and guided her out the door.

"Betcha he's out hunting tomorrow. Don't understand why Crystal is still with that man," said Carole.

"Me neither. I won't take that bet, but he seems to have changed," said Sera.

"In what way?" asked Edie.

"He's less rough around the edges, less of a hothead. I'm guessing marriage calmed the waters," said Sera.

"You mean sex anytime he wants it," said Carole.

"Yeah, he was hot to trot when he was younger. Edie, what's that tune you're humming?" asked Sera.

"Didn't know I was humming. You two ready to go?"

"Yes. Am I meeting you at the church tomorrow?" asked Carole.

"Yes," replied Edie.

"What about after the funeral? You still on for the afternoon?" Carole continued.

"What are you two planning?" asked Sera.

"Looking for garage sales treasures tomorrow," said Carole. "Want to come?"

"No, thanks, I don't need to bring any more secondhand stuff into my house. I'm trying to get rid what I've got," Sera said.

"I said I'd go, so count me in," said Edie.

TWENTY-NINE

EDIE PICKED UP the phone on the first ring. It was the middle of the night and an automatic reflex to keep from waking Hillary. She remembered too late that Hillary wasn't there, it could have gone to voice mail. Hell, she wasn't asleep anyway; the Klein visitation kept playing in her head. She answered the phone. "This is Edie Swift."

"Edie," a soft voice sobbed, "I'm sorry Edie, I didn't know who to call. This is Mariah . . . Mariah Collins."

"Mariah, where are you? Are you safe?" The questions came naturally to Edie. Once a cop, always a cop, Edie thought.

"I'm at the hospital."

"Are you okay?"

"I don't know. They say I am, but I don't know."

"Then you need to hit the call light for help, one of the nurses or doctors will answer."

"There's one standing next to me."

"Tell her or him what you need."

"You don't understand. I need someone to come and get me. Edie, could you come and get me?"

Edie did a quick run-through of her own situation: no one needed her at home, Phil and Hillary were still at Lorraine's. Edie took a deep breath, "Yes, I will, which hospital are you at?"

"The emergency room in Sun Prairie."

The ER waiting room was packed. The beginning of another long weekend for the staff, Edie guessed. A safety officer recognized Edie and had the nurse buzz her into the care area. Inside the ER, another nurse pointed her to a far corner exam room. Edie knocked, and then entered. The exam room was dimly lit; she barely recognized Mariah, who was curled on the exam table facing the wall.

"Mariah, it's me, Edie Swift." Edie pulled a chair close to the exam table.

"Thanks for coming," said Mariah as she turned to face Edie.

During her patrol days Edie saw her share of bruised and battered faces. Mariah's wasn't the worst she'd seen; at least her head was still attached to her body. Still, for the chief mourner at a funeral later that day, she was a mess.

"Airbags deployed."

"Is there a beginning to this story?"

"Yeah. Crystal called, wanted to talk, I couldn't sleep and needed to talk, so I told her I'd come into the nursing home. I didn't make it. I was T-boned by a drunk."

"Sorry to hear that, but why call me?"

"My family is falling apart over Nick's death. Didn't think they could handle me looking like this," Mariah said, tears running down her cheeks.

Edie handed her a tissue. "Are you going to be admitted to a hospital?"

"No. I want to go home. Edie . . . what am I going to do?"

"Call your parents. They are going to see you. It's better that they see you sooner than later—they'll have some time to adjust before the funeral. Then have them take you home, and you need to put in a full eight hours of sleep."

"Maybe, but what am I going to do?"

"Mariah, I don't understand. What are you going to do about what?"

"They tell me I'm pregnant."

Edie stared at Mariah, another can of worms for this woman to handle. She must be one of those people who never seem to be given a break. "You're going to call—"

"They wanted to do lots of x-rays, but when they told me I'm pregnant, I wouldn't let them do the x-rays. It's my baby too. It's not just Nickie's."

In Edie's assessment, Mariah needed watching over. She needed to stay in the hospital. "Maybe you should stay for observation."

"No. I don't want to. I'd probably miss Nick's funeral, and that family of his would be center stage—they've wanted that forever, and they would ruin it all. I'm not going to give them that chance."

"It seems to me you've made a decision to not follow medical advice, then want me to make the rest of the decisions for you. I don't like that. But I don't like that you seem to be taking on the world by yourself more. And since you're refusing to spend the night at the hospital, I'll see what I can do. I'll be back in a moment," Edie said. She stepped into the hallway, pulled her cell from her back pocket, scrolled to Carole's number, punched it, and hoped that Carole hadn't drunk too much of Ray's home brew and would answer the phone.

THIRTY

EDIE WAS AT the Troutbeck church early. She selected a spot in the far corner of the last pew of the church—the best place from which to watch the mourners enter and wait for the service for Nicholas Klein to begin. It wasn't the best seat in the house for her purposes—the pulpit would have been better.

Nick's family was lined up in the center aisle to receive the last mourners. Mariah's family stood between them and Mariah. Crystal sat nearby, in the first pew, as support for Mariah. Edie saw the historian sitting at the piano jotting notes. Damn, why didn't she think of sitting there?

Carole leaned over Edie's shoulder, "See that family in the fifth pew on the right? Professional mourners, they're regulars at funerals. They really want a free meal, maybe that's why they got money in the bank."

"How do you know this stuff?"

"I'm a stylist, my ears are open and my mouth is shut, most of the time."

"Hear any gossip about Nick?"

"Nope, check me later, though."

"How'd Mariah do?"

"Cried herself to sleep, poor girl. Don't want to be in her shoes."

"Crystal's here, where's Lee?"

"Typical Lee Mitchell. Sera must be going senile if she thinks Lee Mitchell's settled down."

The funeral rituals began. The casket was placed in the aisle—center stage. The mourning families were ushered to the back, from which they would make their entrance. The music started. "Amazing Grace" had been chosen. The families walked in, some sobbing. Gasps were heard throughout the church as Mariah, with her battered face, entered, her head held high, her face visible to all. The families took their seats. The music stopped. The minister took over and brought everyone's attention back to the purpose of the day—a reminder that this life was temporary, and that it was time to say good-bye to Nicholas Klein, a child of God. Holly Sundby wasn't in church. Neither was Lee Mitchell.

After the service, Edie walked with the other mourners as they followed the hearse to the cemetery behind the church. She stood at the edge of the crowd, watching the mourners' reaction. None of the emotions seemed out of place: tears, withdrawn stares, and eyes wandering over the cemetery. They all seemed appropriate to Edie. She, too, was drawn to her own thoughts. It was a beautiful day, better, she thought, for birthing a baby, getting married, rather than a funeral. It was a day made for beginnings, not endings.

After the last song was sung, the last handful of dirt dropped on the coffin, the last rose placed, the mourners drifted back toward the church. A few stopped at the bench where Nick had died, shook their heads, then moved on. Mariah's family gathered round her as they walked past that site. They did not stop. Crystal stopped at Mamie Brown's grave, she knelt—it seemed to Edie that she was searching for something. Edie started toward Crystal to see what was happening. Harold Acker, with his cane in one hand, and the other holding onto Sera Voss, got there first. Crystal stood up. Harold handed his cane to Sera, reached for Crystal, and pulled her closer. That got Edie's attention. She moved next to the group, stood beside Sera. They stood in silence. Though less than an inch apart, each was a world apart enveloped in their separate grief.

Harold broke the spell. "Crystal, is that Mamie Robin's perfume you're wearing?"

"Yes, it is. Cristalle, still my favorite perfume." Crystal's hand went to her throat, but whatever talisman she sought wasn't there. She put her hand in her coat pocket.

"You're not wearing the necklace," said Harold.

"No, probably lost it at the nursing home. The women residents all loved that daisy necklace. One of them probably pulled it off when I struggled to get her into bed. I miss it. That and the perfume were all I had left of Mamie Robin."

"Don't worry, I have another necklace just like it at home that you can have. Did you know my Mamie and I bought those necklaces and the perfumes for Mamie Robin to give to you girls? She was so young when she got married, couldn't even afford gifts for her attendants."

"You bought our perfume too?"

"Yup."

"That was sweet of you, thank you."

"It was my Mamie that was the sweet one. But it was the least we could do for one of our little sweethearts."

Silence crept in again.

Moments later, it was Crystal who broke it. "I'm hungry." One of life's clarion calls.

Harold and Sera looked at Crystal, and smiled. Harold took Crystal's arm and the three walked back to the church buildings.

Edie watched them go. *I want to see that necklace. I need to talk with Harold. This is Crystal's weekend to work. Tomorrow should be soon enough to visit Harold.* For Edie, that was a hard fact to swallow; she was beginning to know the habits of each of the residents of Troutbeck. What would she do next? Walk into their houses unannounced?

THIRTY-ONE

EDIE LOOKED AT her watch, Phil and Hillary were late. Lorraine probably insisted that they stay for one more meal, and Phil could never say no to his mother. Five minutes later she looked at her watch, again. Carole was late. Lateness was something that had always annoyed Edie. If Carole was any later, she'd call Matilda and cancel the babysitting job. A better plan would be to call Carole and cancel the garage sale expedition. She felt in her jeans pocket, no cell phone. Oh, yeah, it was in the house being charged. This afternoon she was too lazy to get up, all she wanted to do was sit on her front step. Waiting for Carole was a good excuse for doing nothing. But it bugged her; why had she agreed to let Carole drive? Why in hell did she agree to go to garage sales with Carole? As far as she was concerned, garage sales were worthless, and the time was better spent at home. She really needed to spend more time with Hillary. Another reason to hate garage sales: time away from her daughter. What could she possibly find at garage sales that would interest her? It was keeping her from visiting Harold and seeing that necklace. Knowing that it existed was bothering her. She wanted to see it now. She hoped that she hadn't miscalculated Crystal's work schedule. Could she get to Harold's house before Crystal? This morning she knew nothing about that necklace. Now, she was obsessing about it. If Carole didn't show up soon, she'd cancel the whole thing.

Carole laying on the horn pulled Edie from her thoughts. "Get off your butt, we've got to move it. The best deals are already gone." Edie got into the back seat. "Edie, remember Bridget Briggs? You met her last week at the salon," Carole said as she backed out of Edie's driveway.

"I remember, the high school principal."

"That's only part of what I do," replied Bridget.

"What else do you do?" asked Edie.

"I'm a botanist by training; I propagate Wisconsin native plants. Also I'm a great cook, mother, wife, to name a few of the other things I do."

"You are a busy woman," said Edie.

"Gotta make hay while the sun shines."

"You can always sleep when it rains," said Carole.

"That must be the PG version of the saying," said Edie.

"With all that Bridget does, she doesn't have time for sex," said Carole.

"Speak for yourself," said Bridget.

"Where are we going?" Edie asked, hoping that would keep Carole and Bridget from asking about her sex life.

"Got the route all mapped out," said Bridget.

"Looking for something in particular?" asked Edie.

"I'm looking for local yearbooks. Some of my school's collection developed legs," said Bridget.

"Kids stealing old yearbooks! Why?" asked Carole.

"I don't know. I'm a principal, I don't have keys to kids' logic."

"You think they're logical?" Carole asked

"In their own minds, they are," Bridget replied.

Edie brought the subject back to garage sales; she was tired of teenagers. "Anything else you're looking for?"

"Anything that piques my interest. I'm not into collecting anything in particular, except native plants. What about you, Edie?

"Checking the town out. Never knew there was a Columbus, Wisconsin, till Phil and I moved to Troutbeck."

"Where'd you move from?" asked Bridget.

"Madison."

"That explains a lot. Every person I've ever met from Madison had blinders on, nothing else exists. That city is either golden or the Emerald City," said Bridget.

"See, Edie, she thinks there's something weird about Madison, too," said Carole.

"You two are jealous because you can't claim it as your hometown," said Edie.

"What's so special about Moscow on Mendota?" Bridget asked

"Everything. To paraphrase Hemingway, Madison is a moveable feast," said Edie.

"And you can tell us all about it on the way back home," said Carole, parking in front of Fireman's Park. "This is the first place, everyone out."

"What do you mean first place? I thought you were kidding when you said you had a route mapped out. How many are we going to?" Edie asked as she closed the car door.

"As many as we can fit in. There are three within walking distance from here," said Bridget. "Remember, I got a map of places to stop. Want to see it?"

"Really? You're not kidding?" Edie said in disbelief.

Carole and Bridget looked at each other. "We've got a virgin!"

"What?" said Edie, stepping away from them.

"Tell us, how many garage sales have you been to in your life?" Carole asked.

"None."

"That makes you a virgin. Bridget, how should we celebrate Edie's baptism into the wonders of garage sales?"

"I'm not sure I've ever met that type of virgin before. Let's see, drinks afterwards. Cram as many sales in as possible. How much money do you have on you?" said Bridget.

"Sixty," replied Edie.

"First rookie mistake, never tell us how much money you have," said Carole.

"Carole, can your car hold that much stuff?" asked Bridget.

"Depends on what we buy," said Carole as she assessed the load-bearing capacity of her car.

Edie ignored the feeling that she should sprint home. These were, after all, her neighbors. It was probably best to put on a smile and look past their deranged joy in garage sales. But at the end of her initiation, Edie had bought three bags of clothes and an assortment of toys that Carole and Bridget assured her Hillary would grow into. Edie was happy to end the day at the Troutbeck Bar and Gas Shop.

Carole ordered the first round of beer—whatever was on tap. Edie took a few sips as she watched Carole and Bridget toss back their beers and order more, then pushed the glass away. "Fill'em up, Mike, we're celebrating the end of Edie's virginity," said Carole.

Mike looked at Edie, who shrugged her shoulders at Carole's comments, then shook her head no, she didn't want a drink—she had just appointed herself the designated driver. Mike placed more beers in front of Carole and Bridget; this time they only downed a quarter of their drink. While her friends drank, Edie paged through the yearbooks that Bridget had insisted on dragging into the bar with them. Edie was happy to have them. In her experience, drunks weren't that much fun to talk to. Edie looked up from the yearbooks when she heard the door open. God, she thought, I've joined the ranks of the regulars. It was Crystal Mitchell. Edie smiled at her, tried to ignore Carole and Bridget, and then went back to looking through the books.

Crystal walked up to the bar and stood next to Edie. "Do you know where Mike is? I need a receipt."

Edie shrugged her shoulders. "I think he's in the storeroom."

Crystal looked at the other women at the bar. "Is that Mrs. Briggs? Is she drunk?" said Crystal. "I didn't know high school principals got drunk."

"I know! Who'da thunk that teachers and principals were people," said Edie.

"No one. God, I'm drunk. Someone give me a glass of water," Bridget said, putting her head on the bar. "And you, little girl," she continued, moving her head to look at Crystal. "You remember that we principals are your pals. Principal ends with pal. That means we're pals forever. Remember that."

"Hairdressers are pals, too, and so are cops. Cops are your pals, too. Ain't that right, Edie? Edie, why are you still a cop after that licking?"

"I like the job, and I'm good at it." Edie leaned over the bar, found a glass, filled it with water, and plopped it in front of Bridget. "Bridget, didn't know you were a cadbury."

"Never tried that, give me a shot of it," said Carole.

"It's not something to drink. That word comes from another country. It's someone who gets drunk on less than a glass of alcohol," said Edie. She looked around for Mike Erdmann; he was nowhere in sight.

"Edie, you are so intelligent. Get me some more water, please."

Crystal took a clean bar napkin and began to write a note. "I really need to get to work. Edie, would you give this note to Mike? It's about needing a receipt." The storeroom door slammed shut. They all turned to look. "He's back, I'll tell him myself." Crystal stopped writing, but didn't throw the note away. She asked Mike for a receipt. Casually, she opened the top yearbook, placed her note inside, closed the book, then pushed the stack of yearbooks to Edie and left.

Edie wondered if anyone else had been watching Crystal's activities. She continued to watch Crystal as she got into her car and drove away. It was time for her to go home, too. "Carole, Bridget, time to get you two drunks home."

"I'm not drunk. This is weak compared to Ray's brews," said Carole as she slid off her stool, grabbing the bar to steady herself.

"I'm sure you're not. Carole, give me your car keys." Edie held out her hand, waited until Carole fumbled through her purse, then found the keys in her jean pocket. "You two follow me." She picked up the yearbooks, took out Crystal's note, reading it on the way to the car. *I need to talk to you* was all that was written. She checked the other side. Yup, that was all that was written. There were no specifics about the where, when, or why. Edie was real curious about the why. But more curious about when Crystal would ever show up for an appointment.

166

THIRTY-TWO

EDIE WALKED BACK to her house, carrying her garage sale treasures, after safely returning the inebriated Bridget and Carole to their homes. She saw Matilda and another girl sitting on her front doorstep. Edie dropped her packages in front of the girls, "Hi, girls, when did you get here?"

"Sage and I've been sitting here for a while," said Matilda.

"Did you knock? Phil should be home."

"Yes, and we used the doorbell, too. No one answered."

Edie set the bags down, then looked at her watch, Phil and Hillary were supposed to be at home. Edie pulled out her house keys and opened the door, inviting the girls in. "Come on in girls. We'll wait for Phil inside. I'm sure he and Hillary will be back any moment." Matilda and Sage picked up Edie's bags and carried them into the house. "Thanks, you can set those bags near the couch. I'll text Phil to see what the holdup is," Edie said as she walked into the kitchen to get her phone. She left the phone on the charger as she texted Phil.

"She knows how to text!" Sage whispered to Matilda.

Matilda whispered back, "Yeah, I'm surprised. Maybe every old person doesn't need our help."

Matilda and Sage were sitting on the couch when Edie returned to the living room. "Sorry Phil and Hillary aren't here. While we're waiting, can I get you girls anything to drink? Water, pop, lemonade?'

"Nothing for me," said Sage.

"Just water for me," said Matilda.

Edie returned with a glass of water for each girl. She sat in the armchair nearest the couch, then held out her hand to Sage. "Sage, I'm Edie Swift." Sage shook Edie's hand. Limp, thought Edie, maybe she's shy. "What have you two been doing with your weekend?"

"Driving around," said Matilda. "I told you, Sage comes up here whenever she can. She likes getting out of her house and visiting me. We've been through Columbus, into Madison to the mall. We're thinking of going up to Devil's Lake tomorrow."

"Sage, it's nice your parents let you come up here," said Edie.

"Sure," said Sage.

"How can you afford the gas for all those trips?"

"I babysit," said Sage.

"You must sit every night of the week," said Edie.

"Mostly," said Sage.

"Just like I told you, she's good with kids," said Matilda.

"Excuse me, I'll see if I've got a message yet," said Edie, going into the kitchen. A moment later, she was back with her phone. "No messages, and my calls are going to voice mail."

"Maybe your husband's phone is off," Sage offered.

Matilda leaned over and whispered in Sage's ear, "She's not married."

"You're not married! And you've got a kid! That happens to old people?" Sage said.

"Yes. And I'm not a teenager. And I have a job to support that child. And I have good family to help me with my child," said Edie.

"You're lucky," said Sage.

"Your parents would help out, if that happened to you," said Matilda.

"Not in a million, trillion years would they help me," said Sage.

Edie studied Sage for a moment. She didn't know the kid—would Sage pick up on language subtleties, or should she be blunt? "Are you pregnant?" Blunt it was.

"No," said Sage, defiantly returning Edie's steady gaze.

Edie broke the awkward silence that followed. "Phil hasn't answered any of my messages, don't know when he'll be back. You can go home. I'll pay you for the time you were supposed to be with Hillary. What's the current rate for babysitting?"

"You're a newbie, aren't you?" asked Sage.

"You're supposed to ask the other mothers what they pay, not us. And most of those mothers would pay whatever we asked so they could get away from their kids," said Matilda.

The girls looked at each other, telegraphing some message. Matilda answered, "Do you mind if we hang out here for a while?"

"No, but there really isn't anything for you to do here."

"We could play euchre," said Sage.

"No we can't, we need four players," said Matilda.

"Sorry, I don't know the game," said Edie.

"You never played it? I thought everyone in Wisconsin played euchre," said Matilda.

"Not in my group of friends," said Edie, thankful that no one asked her what card games she and her friends had played.

"Sage, we can play with three. Since she doesn't know the game, we'll just play with the cards face up until Ms. Swift catches on, and I'll play two hands till then," said Matilda.

"Please call me Edie. Matilda, are you a good teacher?"

"She taught me, and I've taught my friends," said Sage.

"And I've taught all the younger kids on the school bus," said Matilda.

"You have time to play on the bus?" said Edie.

"Yeah, it's a forty-five minute ride to school. I'd rather play cards than do homework. Do you have a deck of cards?" said Matilda.

"Sure," said Edie, going into the kitchen to get the deck out of the catch-all drawer.

Matilda and Sage followed her.

"Where do you want to play? The counter okay?" asked Edie.

"Works best to play at a table," said Matilda.

Edie handed her the deck. Matilda separated the nine and above cards, then shuffled them while instructing Sage and Edie on the game. "Sage, you and Edie, you'll be partners. So, sit across from each other. That's the way it's usually done, Ms. Swift, but not always."

"You can call me Edie."

"Now, I deal five cards to each player in two passes. Three cards are given to each player on the first pass, then second pass, two cards," said Matilda.

"What about the leftover cards?" asked Edie.

"They're called the blind," said Matilda, dealing the cards, then setting the blind near her, and turning the top card over. "Okay, everyone turn your cards over."

Edie and Sage followed her orders. "The top card of the blind is a heart. If it's picked up, then all the cards in that suit are trump. The jack in the trump suit is the highest card, the jack in the same colored card, in this case diamonds, is the next highest. Then it goes ace, king, queen, ten, and nine. Got it?"

"Matilda says you're a cop," said Sage.

"Yes, I'm a detective with the Dane County Sheriff's Office."

"Do you like your job?" asked Sage.

"Yes."

"Play proceeds to the left. Edie, you have the highest card, the jack of hearts, also known as the right bower. Your partner has the second highest card, the jack of diamonds, also known as the left bower. You have a decent hand. Since I'm playing two hands, I'd order me to pick up the ten," said Matilda.

"Okay, pick up the card," said Edie.

Matilda picked up the card, then put one of her discarded card face down on the blind. "Okay, hearts are now trump. I'm sorry, Edie, do you know what trump means?"

Edie tried to keep a smile off her face. "Yes."

"Remember, the play goes clockwise. Edie, you lead off, start with your jack of hearts. The rest of us have to follow suit, if we can. This means you win this trick."

"Who taught you how to play?" asked Edie.

"The old women at church, they even let me win sometimes while I was learning. But they don't do that now, they're cutthroats now. I can only win if I play well."

"How'd you become a cop?" asked Sage, throwing down the ace of hearts.

"Do you want to know about the education it takes to become a cop, or do you mean why did I become a cop?" asked Edie.

"I guess I mean why," said Sage.

"When I was in college, a friend got hurt. I talked her into calling the campus police. Two officers answered the call, one was a moron, and the other was helpful—she kept in touch with my friend throughout the case. Let my friend know what was happening every step of the way. I wanted to do what that cop did," said Edie.

"What happened to your friend?" asked Sage.

Matilda finished playing that hand. "Edie, you took that trick. Throw down another card."

Edie threw down the nine of hearts. "My friend was raped."

Sage gasped. The game stopped.

"What happened?" asked Sage.

"She was walking back alone from the library late at night."

"She shouldn't have done that," said Sage.

Matilda finished playing the hand by herself.

"That might have been stupid, but she shouldn't have been raped," said Edie.

"What was she wearing?" asked Sage.

"Edie, you and your partner won a couple of points," said Matilda as she gathered the cards, shuffled them, and dealt another round.

"Rape isn't about what you're wearing. It's about domination, hatred, rage, hurting someone. It's not about how you look. Sometimes it is being in the wrong place at the wrong time," said Edie.

"But if we don't give them a chance—" Sage began.

"We could all stay inside and do nothing," said Edie.

"That doesn't stop them," said Sage.

Edie took a long look at Sage. Where did that knowledge come from? "No, it doesn't, and it would be a very boring existence. We'd be prisoners in our own homes."

"Are you two interested in playing this game?" asked Matilda. No one answered her. She stopped playing and listened.

"But what can a cop do to end the rapes?" asked Sage.

"We educate girls and boys, women and men. For those assaults that we can't stop, we track down the bad guy. It helps to set the world a little more right."

"What does it take to become a cop?" asked Matilda.

"There's lots of paperwork. Interviews. The police academy. Physical fitness. And a steadfast heart."

"A steadfast heart? What does that mean?" asked Sage.

"These days we cops have become like lawyers, everyone hates us until they need us. So, as a cop you've got to know that what you are doing is right and benefits the community. If you do that, you can withstand all the negative things people throw at you. That's what a steadfast heart means."

"There seems to be a lot of bad cops these days," said Sage.

"I agree with you. There are some people who shouldn't be cops. Either their head isn't screwed on right, or they think that a badge lets you do anything. We are not above the law. You hope the higher-ups in the department weed the bad ones out before they harm someone."

Matilda's phone rang. She pulled it from her back pocket. "It's my mother, we probably need to get home." She put it back in her pocket without answering it. She and Sage got up from the table.

"Matilda, could we stay here for supper?" asked Sage.
Matilda looked at Edie.

"As long as it's okay with your mother. Since Phil and Hillary aren't here, I'd like the company."

Matilda called her mother back and got the okay from her. She and Sage helped Edie fix the meal.

Near the end of supper Sage wanted to know some moves to protect herself, "You know, just in case I'm walking alone."

Edie suggested that they wait for a bit until their food had settled. She stoked the fire while the girls washed the dishes. And before they left for home, she demonstrated a few self-defense moves. "Of course, the more you practice these maneuvers, the better you will get." Matilda and Sage were almost out the door before Edie remembered her promise to pay them. "Wait a moment. I said I'd pay you for the time." She took a wad of bills from her front pants pocket, and gave a five to each girl. "You never told me what sitters earn these days."

"More than this, but we'll take it because we didn't really do anything," said Sage.

Edie didn't mention that the girls had eaten her food, grilled her about being a detective, played a game of cards, and learned some self-defense.

Edie followed the girls to the front door and saw Matilda slip Sage her five, then watched them until they were home.

THIRTY-THREE

"GIVE ME BACK my blankets, Sunday is my day of rest," Edie growled, grabbing the covers and pulling them back over her head.

"Not when you have a kid," said Phil, pulling the covers away from Edie. "And not when you're meeting your boss at the firing range."

Phil's voice penetrated her fog of sleep. Edie sat up, alert. "Where the hell have you been?"

"Watch your language, Hillary's in the next room and awake," said Phil.

Edie got out of bed and closed their bedroom door. "Answer the question."

"I don't remember what it was."

"Don't plead brain-dead with me."

"I was at my mother's."

"Doing what?"

"Thinking."

"About what?"

"Us."

"You thought about us all weekend and yet you didn't call or text me. How considerate of you. I trust you, to hell and back, but next time you refuse to respond to me, or keep my kid away from me, I'll accuse you of kidnapping, then I'll hunt you down, and if you are still alive—divorce you or worse."

"You can't divorce me, we're not married."

"Shut up. I want to take away something positive from this emotional rollercoaster I've been on since yesterday."

"I can't help you find it now, you gotta meet Gracie in thirty-five minutes."

"Damn, I forgot about Gracie!" Edie shouted, jumping out of bed. "What time is it?"

"Seven twenty-five."

"I have time to get to the range. I'll get breakfast afterward," said Edie, stripping off her long johns and wriggling into some jeans, hooking up a sports bra, and pulling on a sweatshirt.

"I brought you a breakfast sandwich and coffee."

"Is that a peace offering?"

Edie took her gun from the locked box that she kept on the top shelf of her closet, way in the back, checked it, and then secured it in her belt holster.

"It can be, if you want it to be. I never argue with a woman holding a gun," said Phil, as he walked out of their bedroom.

Phil came back with the coffee and sandwich. "What's your plan for today?'

"Shooting range with Gracie, talk with Harold Acker, give Bridget her books back, and talk with the historian."

"Where does Hillary fit in?'

"Nap time. I can take a nap with her."

"She needs more of your presence than that. She had you all winter, now she doesn't see you much. How about playing with her?"

"I'll take over this afternoon, promise."

"Good, I've got stuff to work on at the shop." He handed her the travel mug of coffee, took the crumb-filled plate from her, and then practically shoved her out the door.

"I can feel the love. What happened to the spirit of peace?" Edie shouted back.

"You'll be late. Don't speed, this is Troutbeck."

"I won't get a ticket; I'll get an escort when they find out who I'm meeting."

"I thought a quiet day at home would do you good. Boy was I wrong. Go," said Phil, slamming the door.

Edie looked at her watch as she drove into the shooting range parking lot. No problem, she had minutes to spare, she thought. But Gracie was waiting for her at the door, with ear and eye protectors for herself in hand.

Deputy Bellinger checked them in, looked over their guns, gave each three magazines of blanks, and then assigned them to the furthest bunker from the building. Edie grabbed ear and eye protectors on the way out to the range.

Halfway to the bunker, Edie stopped. "Damn, the bastard's tracking me."

"Who is?" asked Gracie

"Phil."

"Why do you think that?"

"One of the last things he said this morning as I left was about me having a quiet day yesterday."

"Maybe he was talking about you not working."

"But I was, at least part of the day."

"Doesn't add up to him tracking you. Need more evidence than that."

"I left my phone and car at home yesterday."

"Then he might be tracking you. What's the big deal? You walk into some stores with your cell on, they track you. The NSA and who knows what other government agencies do that. It's been going on for a long time. Bush 2 did it. Nixon did. I've heard J. Edgar Hoover did it. God only knows who else was doing it. And I'm sure that those government agencies are jealous of all the Internet companies, because we voluntarily let them invade our privacy. When was the last time you did a search on the web? 'Cause next time you get on, there'll be ads for that product popping up all over the place. Internet hackers track us. I read that some of our products, like baby monitors, track us. And I track my kids. Do you want me to keep going?"

"No, and I'm not a kid. Do your kids know you're tracking them? I know about the Internet trackings. I can ignore them. But I didn't know that Phil was tracking me. What happened to mutual trust? That is what is most disturbing—the loss of trust."

"Yes, my children know about my keeping tabs on them, helps keep them on the straight and narrow. So, you're not concerned about anonymous invasions of your privacy while you are on the Internet, but you are concerned about the man who loves you and wants to keep you safe. Maybe that's all he wants to do, keep you safe. What are you going to do about it?"

"You don't need to lecture me about Phil's noble intentions. His actions put me on the same level as a child. It puts me back in the time when a woman was either her father's property or husband's. Haven't we moved past that? And what I am going to do about it is first make certain that he's tracking me, and then I'll punt."

Gracie started laughing. "Don't use his head for the ball."

"That is too far north from where I'd be aiming."

"Don't call me if he presses charges. Let's move on to a safer topic. How's your case going?" Gracie asked.

"Okay, got a few leads that I'm following up. Still want to connect with the victim's friend, Lee—he doesn't seem to have any time these days."

"Do you have a case without him?"

"Nothing concrete, and I don't know if he will add anything to it either."

"What's keeping him from talking to you?"

"Hunting."

"Always something to hunt around here. Think he'll talk to a man?"

"Worth a shot."

"Any suspects?"

"Lots. Each interview leads to another suspect or two."

"Who are they?"

"There's the wife, a few mistresses, maybe their husbands and or boyfriends."

"You convinced it's one of them?"

"Not yet, they are all still maybes, but at the moment the wife is the best possibility"

"What about the Brown case you were asking about?"

"I'll work on that one after the Klein case."

On reaching the bunker, they laid their guns on the stand, Edie put up the targets, and then stepped back behind the stand. She and Gracie put on their eye and ear protectors, loaded a magazine, popped it into the gun, flipped off their safety, assumed a firing stance, and then fired until their magazine was depleted, dropped it from the gun, slammed the next one in place, and fired. And repeated. With their bullets spent, they placed their guns on the stand before Edie took down their targets.

"You're listing to the left, but still on target. Not bad for not practicing since October," said Gracie.

"You shredded the center. Ever have to shoot someone?"

"Yes. Once."

"Could you do it again?"

"Yes. I hope and pray I never have to shoot anyone. I still get nightmares about it, on occasion. My cop voice is usually effective in stopping people."

And being a six-foot black woman with a badge and pistol helps, thought Edie.

"Want to go again?" asked Gracie.

"Love to, but we're out of ammo."

"Time for me to go home, too."

"Gracie, you were dead on with your shots. Why come out with me?"

"See if you're ready. If you're needed in an explosive situation, can we count on you? Will you have our backs?"

"I've been cleared."

"Physically, but are you ready for the mental challenge? 'Cause, Edie, right or wrong, we cops are taking a lot of heat today. And we don't need anyone standing on the sidelines."

"Yes, I'm ready. Are you ready to get rid of the bad apples?"

"Yes, we keep on weeding them out. But some still creep in. Train as much as we do, you never know how people will react in a real situation. It's good to know that you're ready for the job, but I still want you to talk with someone in the peer support group."

"When I have time," said Edie. Gracie didn't need to know everything that was going on in her life. She'd tell her in her own good time.

"Make time. And make time to stop and see me and my family."

"Love to, but not today."

"Work?"

"Yes."

"Don't you need some downtime?"

"Had plenty of that. This can't wait, gotta see a man about a necklace."

THIRTY-FOUR

EDIE'S BUTT WAS cold from sitting on Harold Acker's step as she waited for him to come home from church. She stood up, walked down his driveway to the road, looked up toward the church. No one was milling around the church doors, no cars were parked on the side of the road across from the church, everyone seemed to be gone. What was taking him so long to get home?

She looked back at the stoop. It would be cold by now, and she should never have left it. Edie went back to the cement step and parked her butt there. Better a cold ass than a missed opportunity. The line of crocuses along Harold's house caught Edie's attention, they looked so delicate. How did they survive the recent cold winter blast? She expanded her vision and admired how far much of the grass had turned green, taking over the territory once owned by snow. Not long from now the trees would bud, the warm winds would push back the northern winds, and she could shed the winter-weight clothes for a while. A car turning into the driveway pulled Edie from her reverie. Harold was home.

For a moment they stared at each other, and then Harold opened the car door. With one hand on the door to steady himself, he grabbed his cane. With the other, he then pushed himself out of his car, slammed the door shut, and made his way to Edie. "Hope you haven't been waiting long, Mrs. Best."

Edie let it pass, "Please, call me Edie."

"Something I can do for you, Edie?" Harold asked, attempting to stretch to reach his former height.

"Interested in seeing that necklace you were talking about with Crystal yesterday."

"Mamie Robin's?"

"Yes, the one from her wedding. Is it a daisy necklace?"

"Yes it is. I've promised it to Crystal."

"May I see it?"

Harold was quiet for a moment. "Sure, you can look at it, come on in."

Edie held the storm door open for Harold as he fumbled with his keys. As they entered the kitchen, its stale air hit her. Looking around, she noticed the place was immaculate. She wondered which Troutbeck woman cleaned for him this week. She followed him into the bedroom—this was more like it. There was dust on the furniture, clothes on the chair, the bed was unmade, and the carpet looked as if it needed vacuuming.

"Sorry about the mess, I haven't had a lady in here since my Mamie died. Don't let those women come in here. In this room, I do the cleaning."

Edie looked around. Except for the messiness, it had a woman's touch. "Did your wife decorate this?"

"Not hard to tell she loved lavender." Harold walked over to the antique marble-topped dresser with a jewelry box set to one side, an aging photo of two young people dressed in their wedding best on the other. Harold opened his wife's jewelry box, took out the last of Mamie Robin's daisy necklaces, and then handed it to Edie. "My Mamie and I bought it for our Mamie Robin's wedding.

She didn't have any money to buy her bridesmaids a gift," said Harold, watching Edie examine his precious memory. "It's still in its original wrapper. Safe."

Edie held the packaged necklace in the palm of her hand—it was a young girl's vision of loveliness and a match for the one she found in the cemetery. "It's very pretty. Tell me about Mamie Robin."

"She was young." Harold pointed to the wall covered with family photos. "The one in the middle is from Mamie Robin's wedding. Sweet thing, she loved coming over to help my Mamie and me. The house seemed to burst with energy when she was here." Harold pulled a handkerchief from his back pocket and wiped the tears from his cheeks.

"Harold, would you like to sit down?"

"I sit too much these days, but I would love a cup of tea." He walked out of the room.

Edie followed him into the kitchen. "I took you for a coffee-drinking man."

"I am, except on Sundays. Mamie enjoyed tea after church. I always joined her. When I sit down with my tea on Sundays, I feel like Mamie's sharing one with me. I miss her, she was my angel in disguise. I could never figure out why she stayed with me when the only job I could get was being a bouncer down at the Lower Bottom nudie places. An angel she was. Is." Harold wiped a tear from his cheek.

"Let me make you a cup." Edie placed the necklace on the counter where she could keep an eye on it. She put fresh water into the teakettle, placed it on the stove, and then scrounged through the cupboards for tea.

"Be obliged if you had one with me," said Harold, easing himself into a chair at the kitchen table.

"Can't refuse an offer like that." Edie took out another cup. She placed the orange pekoe tea bags in the cups, and set the cups near the stove. On a plate, she arranged the cookies that she found during her rummaging, and then set it in front of Harold. Edie sat down at the table with the daisy necklace in her hand and laid it in front of Harold. "What do you remember about the day Mamie Robin died?"

"I don't like those memories. Our world shut down that day."

"I understand. What kind of day was it? Rainy? Clear? Mild?"

"It was summer, the sun rose orangey pink, there were a few clouds in the sky. The day promised to be a scorcher."

"What did you have for breakfast?"

"Toast, two strips of bacon, two eggs over easy, coffee."

"How do you remember that?"

"It's what I always had for breakfast. Mamie tried to get me to eat differently, but I wouldn't eat anything else, even when she fixed something different for me. She'd end up throwing that stuff away. My Mamie got her way most of the time, but not for breakfast. I was stubborn."

"What else do you remember?"

"The sirens, lots of them. Sandy, our daughter, telling us about our Mamie Robin. Tears rolled like rivers down Sandy's cheeks. The sadness. The fear. The emptiness."

The teakettle whistled. Edie poured the hot water into the cups, and then set them on the table. She waited for Harold to pick up the conversation.

"That was the day everyone locked their doors. Used to be you'd open a friend's door, yell out your name, and then walk in. That stopped, most people never went back to the old ways, and especially not after Tom Brown was cleared. There was a feeling that any stranger or even one of us could have done that to Mamie Robin. We didn't want to be the next victim." Harold took a sip of his tea. "Too bad Tom Brown didn't do it; we could've gone back to our old ways. But it's too late now."

"It's hard not to be scared when something like that happens in a closely knit community. Logical thinking usually gives way to passion. Why was Tom Brown ruled out as a suspect?"

"Heard that he was at work and everyone there could vouch for him."

"Mamie Robin and Tom lived in Troutbeck, right?"

"Just outside the village. A dump, but it was close to family and it was all they could afford."

"Which house is that?"

"Burned to the ground a few years ago. Why these questions?"

"I'm always intrigued by unsolved crimes. Who do the people of Troutbeck think did it?"

"At first, Tom Brown. Then each other. We'd talk about it at church gatherings, but as the years went past, we stopped. It's like they all forgot."

"Sounds sad. Let me tell you about something I've learned in my years as a cop . . . people remember, but they need to get on with their lives."

"My Mamie said the same thing."

Edie and Harold sipped their tea, ate a cookie. They could have turned to stone for all the silence and thoughts of painful years that hung around them.

Edie wasn't going to let that happen, "Harold, may I keep this necklace?"

"I promised it to Crystal."

"I know, but Mamie Robin is interesting me. After Nick's case is closed, I'd like to look into your grand-daughter's case. A new set of eyes is always good."

"Would you?" Harold's shoulders dropped away from his ears, he seemed to sit taller, and a sparkle came to his eyes. It was as if he lost ten years when he heard Edie's suggestion.

"Yes, but after Nick's case is over. May I take the necklace with me?"

"Sure."

"Do you have a clean paper bag, like an unused lunch bag, in the house? I need to keep this necklace safe." Harold pushed himself off his chair, shuffled to the counter, and looked through it until he found a bunch of brown paper lunch bags. He shuffled back to the table, gave the unopened bunch to Edie.

"Keep them, I don't use them anymore."

"One is just fine." Edie dropped the necklace into the bag, wrote date, time, and contents on the outside. "I'll take a second one, thanks." She wrote a receipt for the necklace, and then handed it to Harold. "Keep that in a safe spot."

Harold held the receipt to his heart.

"Harold, who does the town think killed Nick?"

"Accident. Some jerk out shooting in the middle of the night. Ain't no one going to come forward and tell you he's done it."

"Do shootings like that happen often?"

"Throughout the year, though not like it used to."

Edie looked at her watch. "Sorry to leave so soon, but this afternoon is my time with my baby."

"Bring her by sometime. I'd love to hold a little one again."

"I'll keep that in mind. Thanks for the tea."

Edie met Crystal at the end of Harold's drive, they nodded at each other. Edie thought her cold butt was worth it.

THIRTY-FIVE

WHILE HILLARY NAPPED, Edie thought. And the more Edie thought, the more she wanted to put Nick Klein's and Mamie Robin Neuport Brown's cases side by side. But it would have to wait until tomorrow. This afternoon she had mama duty.

Edie stood in the doorway of Hillary's room and watched her baby sleep. Older people were always telling her that she would miss this time. She didn't doubt them, they had been down this road. But there was another job to be done and Edie couldn't spare more time to absorb the precious moments. She gently closed her daughter's door, and then went to the kitchen to bang pots on the stove, and slam cupboard doors, and make supper to relieve the stress of waiting.

Inspiration hit Edie as she slid the no-peek chicken into the oven. The historian. The historian might have information on Mamie Robin. Instead of driving the half hour-plus into Madison to pull the old case files, she could put Hillary into the jogging stroller, then run to the historian's house and maybe have a few questions answered—two birds with one stone. Now, if Hillary would only wake up.

The historian was home and happy to show off the historical records of Troutbeck. The historian took Hillary from Edie, admired her, made funny faces at her, and then carried her as they went upstairs to the record room.

"Did you know that the real estate agent's been showing the vacant store?" asked the historian.

"Haven't heard anything about it. Any idea what the buyer might want to do with it?"

"Lots of gossip, or maybe it's wishful thinking. Some are hoping for a store, but does this village need more than the Bar and Gas?"

Edie noted that there were two rooms on the second floor, one a bedroom, the other, the bigger of the two, was lined with bookcases that went to the ceiling and a small table and two chairs were set in the middle of the room.

"Wow! Is this the whole history of Troutbeck?" Edie asked.

"And the surrounding area," replied the historian. "If it was worth mentioning, it's in these books."

"No privacy back then either?"

"If you wanted a private life, you're living in the wrong place and time," said the historian.

"When was privacy ever of great concern?" asked Edie.

"Maybe when Brandeis argued for it, but probably never. That's a good question to ask the professors at the other end of Highway 151"

The historian flipped on the overhead light. "This used to be my son's room, but with the kids gone, I've made it into the Troutbeck history room. My kids don't like it, but what was I supposed to do—leave it as a shrine to them?"

"How far back do these records go?" Edie asked.

"The area was settled in the 1840s, I think that's when the first record was written."

"You don't know?"

"It was settled by people from Bavaria. I can't read High German, let alone German."

"The university is just down the road, maybe someone there could help translate the books," said Edie, taking a book from a shelf.

"Please put that down. In this room you look with your eyes, not touch with your hands, unless you're wearing the special gloves."

Edie carefully placed the book on the table, took a pair of white cotton gloves from the box that the historian had placed on the table. "Why the gloves?"

"The historian before me said it was to prevent body oils and dirt from getting on the books. Those things will destroy the books. I will not let that happen on my watch. So, if you want to look through these precious books, you will wear those gloves."

"If they're that valuable, they should be where they can be preserved, at the Historical Society or Memorial Library on the UW campus."

"The previous historian entrusted me with these books, if someone wants to read about Troutbeck, they can come and see me. What has Troutbeck been to the rest of the world? A bump in the road. To the people of Troutbeck, this is everything. I can't let this wonderful treasure be shut up where no one who cares about these people will see it."

Edie wondered how many people, besides herself, ever stopped to see the records now. She bit her tongue and got to the subject matter. "What do you have on Mamie Robin Neuport Brown?"

"That is such a sad case. She was so young. Tom Brown still looks lost. All those years wasted," said the historian, pulling three books from the shelves and placing them on the table.

"Must have been a big deal around here."

"It was, but those books aren't only about Mamie, they encompass the years before and after that death."

"Do you have any high school yearbooks?"

"A few, only a few," said the historian with head shaking. "Bridget usually gets to the garage sales before me."

"Any yearbooks from the time Mamie Robin would have been in school?"

"Probably not, it's only children who sell or throw away their parent's treasures, but I'll check." The historian set Hillary in the floor next to Edie.

While Edie waited for the historian to return, she took from the diaper bag the second lunch bag Harold had given her, drew a face, then handed it to Hillary hoping it would distract her for a while. "This is from Mr. Harold, have fun." Hillary turned the bag this way and that, then smashed it together and pulled it apart.

Edie didn't hear her daughter; she was reading about Mamie Robin and Tom Brown's wedding and the days surrounding Mamie Robin's death in the annals of Troutbeck. These were the facts of who said what, where, and when. She couldn't have done any better about statements from reluctant witnesses. Edie thought for a moment—maybe these people would talk to a historian faster than a cop. Most of the statements were of sadness about a joyful life ended by some asshole. Good start, but Edie needed more about that case.

The historian returned with three yearbooks, which she placed in front of Edie. "Hope these help. Sorry I don't have more, I've only started to collect them. See you've already started. If you need me, holler down the stairs. I'll be in the kitchen."

"I do have another question. In the cemetery there's a headstone with three children named Michel on it."

"I know the one. I don't know why there are three Michels in that family. It used to be common to give the name of a deceased child to the next one born of the same gender. I've seen a name used twice, never three times, maybe those children were named after someone very dear to them. Very sad if that's what happened."

"Why did they do that?"

"Don't know in that particular case, but some Germans gave the same saint's name to all their children, then different middle names. It could have been they wanted to keep the name alive and give to the next child that was born. Could also be that two of the three Michels died. Haven't found out about that family yet. I don't think people would do that anymore."

"Thanks."

"Glad to pass on what I've learned about Troutbeck."

After the historian left, Edie looked through the yearbooks, which were filled with promises to be best friends forever, admonishments of "don't ever change," and requests to "remember me" through the years. Edie wondered what type of person put their yearbook in a garage sale—wouldn't it be better to burn it? She paged a little farther and found that in Mamie Robin's year, she was voted the sweetest. And in pictures, Crystal always seemed to be next to her, Mamie Robin's best friend forever.

Edie closed the yearbooks, sat back, and thought back to her own high school years. Friendships faded, but so had the intense rivalries of those years. She wondered how long the friendships and rivalries at Mamie Robin's school had lasted. How many kids, she asked herself, graduated from that high school, but never left. A book dropping on the floor brought Edie back to the present. Hillary was practicing pulling herself to a stand using the bookshelves, Edie quickly picked her up and returned them to the shelves. If Edie's hands were dirty, what were Hillary's like? Would the historian have a heart attack knowing a kid pulled the precious books off the shelf and slobbered on some of the books?

Edie left the historian's house, grateful for some insight into those days, eager for Monday.

THIRTY-SIX

THE HOUSE COULDN'T contain Edie. Whether it was pent-up anger from the weekend, or anticipation of the evening confrontation with Phil, she couldn't tell. She just had to not be in the house. She looked at her daughter, "Let's get out of here, you and me. Any suggestions?" Hillary let out a few delighted sounds as she played in the sunshine. "Don't have any either. Last chance to make your preference known. How about a ride? That's sounds good. Let's see where the car takes us." Edie wrapped her daughter in a blanket, grabbed the diaper bag, then headed out the door.

The car took them north. When they came to a crossroads, their conversation resumed. "You know little one, it's time I see where you and your Granny go. I think this is the way to Hank Erb's place. We are going to pay a visit to his farm." Edie turned left at the crossroads, over some small hills, followed the road as it jogged south until it came to Hank Erb's farm.

Hank Erb's Century Farm sign was in a prominent place near the road. Edie turned onto the long dirt driveway that led back to the farm buildings. She parked the car behind the two-story farmhouse made of cream city brick, unbuckled Hillary, wrapped her in the blanket, and was about to take a self-guided tour when Hank came out of the barn.

"Hi, Edie, what brings you out here?"

"Wanted to see where Aunt Jill and Hillary spent some of their days."

"Not much to see, just a Wisconsin dairy farm. Want to see the barns?"

"Some other time, we're not dressed for it today. Tell me about your farm."

"Not much to tell. It's a century farm, been in my family over a hundred years now."

"With that house, farming must have been good through the years."

"See that small two-story shed? That's the original farmhouse. Keep it to remind me of the hard work it took to make and keep this farm."

"It looks busy around here."

"Getting ready for spring planting."

"How many people work on your farm?"

Herb stopped smiling at Hillary, his back stiffened, "Edie, are you working? Did you come to quiz me on whether my workers were legal?"

"No Herb, I didn't. Not any of my business who you employ. What else can you tell me about the farm?"

"These people are damned good workers, can't get any help from those city kids. Tried a few times to hire them, but they don't know what it means to work. Work seems to be a dirty word to those city kids. Wish those damned politicians would get their heads out of their asses."

"Hank, I didn't mean to hit a soft spot. I'm only here to see where my aunt and my daughter spend part of their day."

"Well, it seems I've rubbed you the wrong way, too."

If Hank could expose a soft spot, so could Edie. "For as long as I can remember, it's only been me and her."

"So she's told me."

"Let's call a truce before a war starts between us."

Edie and Hank stared at each other for a moment. "See that line fence about a quarter of a mile away? That defines the western edge of this farm, it goes south for about a half-mile, to the east it goes to the farm. Some day when I'm planting, you should come for a ride."

"I'd like that. Thanks for your time," said Edie.

Hank stood in the yard until Edie was down the drive.

At least Hank was hardworking, thought Edie. There wasn't much else to go on to assess his character.

THIRTY-SEVEN

THAT NIGHT, AFTER dinner, and Hillary's bath, and her bedtime stories, and with the dishwasher loaded, Edie decided it was time for the talk with Phil. "Hey," she said, "we need to clear the air." Phil was engrossed in a sports broadcast. "Phil." He didn't answer. "Phil." Again no answer. "Phil, what game are you watching?" This time Edie stood between him and the TV.

"Right now the Brewers. Could you move to one side, please?"

"Hillary's asleep. We gottta talk. Are you tracking me?"

"Excuse me, I'm watching the game."

"Read about in tomorrow's paper." Edie held out a GPS tracking device for cars. "Are you tracking me?"

"Where'd you find that?"

"Under my car. Why did you put it there?"

"Because I didn't have time to hardwire your car."

"Are you tracking me?"

Phil took a deep breath, then exploded. "Yes, sue me for wanting to protect you. I want to know where you are every second of the day. Last fall wasn't just about you. You weren't the only victim. Me and our daughter were victims too. We were and are the collateral damage of your beating. I don't want to go through that again.

Every time you've walked out that door this past week, I've wondered if you'd be walking back in. So, yes, I track you. Sue me."

"Thanks for the suggestion. I'll take it up with Brooke." Edie pulled her cell from her back pocket. "Is there an app on my phone too?"

"Yes."

Edie threw the phone at him. "Take it off. Now."

Phil caught the phone Edie had thrown at him. He looked at the phone, and then looked again at Edie. "I almost died last fall along with you. Where would that have left Hillary?" Phil took a deep breath before continuing. "I didn't know how painful sitting on the sidelines watching you work was. I had to do something to ease the tension." Phil stopped for a moment. "I spent this weekend with my mother trying to decide what I wanted to do—stay with you or leave. One beer led to another Saturday night. I woke this morning with a headache . . . not only from the beer, but reliving life with my mother. I came back early because I didn't want to live my mother's way. I can't take her demands anymore. After living with you so many years, I wanted you. Did you know that living with you is hard? You are an unstoppable force."

"Then move out."

"I can't. Living without you is harder."

"Take the app off my phone."

"What are we going to do when Hillary gets older and we track her?

"She's a minor, that's different."

Phil looked down at Edie's cell. "What's your password?"

"You know it. Quit stalling."

Edie watched as Phil removed the app. Then held out her hand for it. "Now give me your phone."

"Why do you want that?" asked Phil.

"Keeping you honest." Edie punched in the code to unlock his phone, and then searched for the GPS monitor app. "I'll have someone at the department check this out."

"You do that," said Phil before he stomped off to bed.

Edie sat on the couch trying to think, then just stared at the darkness outside her window. It didn't help, the anger hadn't dissipated. Soon she stretched out on the couch and waited for sleep to obliterate the ugliness of the day.

THIRTY-EIGHT

MONDAY MORNING THERE was an uneasy truce between Edie and Phil; everyone in the house could feel it. Hillary was cranky until Aunt Jill arrived to scoop her up, and then hurried out the front door with her. After they left, doors, cupboards, and things not nailed down were slammed by Edie. Phil left the house before Edie, slamming the door twice when he left. Edie swore she was going to get a punching bag with her next paycheck and paint Phil's face on it. She too left the house, slamming the door behind her.

At the office, Edie's mood was no better. Deputies felt the anger surging around Edie and began to keep two desks between her and them. They drew straws to see who would approach her about the problems left over from the weekend shift—no one lost. There was a message on her work phone: "Call me at work tonight. Crystal." Okay, thought Edie, what was Crystal going to say that she hadn't already said, or not said? What kind of game was that woman playing? Hide and seek?

Gracie stopped in front of her desk, "My office, now, Detective." Edie slowly followed Gracie. "Close the door." Edie closed the door. "Detective, leave your problems at home."

"He's been tracking me."

"Who?"

"Phil."

"We went over that yesterday. Give it a rest."

"But now I found the evidence."

"So fault him with being overly protective. Same thing my daughters tell me that I am."

"What do you do about it?"

"Nothing. They're my kids. It's my job to keep them safe."

"That's different. They're kids, and I'm not a kid."

"No, you are not. Take that up with Phil, not your coworkers or the public."

"I need to punch something."

"Go to a gym, go anywhere, just get the hell out of here, you're making everyone edgy."

"What am I supposed to do?"

"Go detect something. Now get."

But Edie couldn't leave the building, yet. She had a necklace burning a hole in her pocket. She went to see Ben Harris over with the crime scene investigators.

He had pulled the Nick Klein evidence box as Edie had requested, "Good to see you back on your feet. Heard the news on the bones they found up in the Baraboo range?"

"No."

"They're going to do facial reconstruction. When finished, it can be compared to the description you gave to the facial artist. So, what are you going to add to this box of evidence?"

Edie handed him the paper bag to Ben. "A necklace."

"Doesn't look like your style."

"Never would have been, but it was treasured by Mamie Robin Brown."

"She connected to the case?"

"Don't know yet. But I'd like you to pull her file. I want to see if there's a necklace like this in it."

"And the mystery deepens. Can't you ever get a straightforward case?"

"Where the perpetrator is found at the scene with a smoking gun, or a bloody knee, and gives a full confession?"

"Something along those lines," said Ben.

"Does it ever happen?"

"No, it would make our jobs easier if everyone were a little more honest."

"Then there wouldn't be crime, and then where would we be?"

"Up north fishing."

"Season doesn't open for a few more weeks."

"I'm ready for it."

"There's another necklace in that box, can you take it out for me?"

"Sure, anything you ask. Why don't you take it out?"

"I want a second opinion about those two necklaces."

Ben looked through the evidence box, found the first necklace and took the bag out, then compared the two. "Eyeballing them, they look to be the same, except one is worn and the other is new. Where'd you find them?"

"One in the Troutbeck cemetery, the other at a residence in Troutbeck."

"Connected?"

"Maybe."

"What have you done with the real Edie Swift?"

"Nothing. Why?"

"You're full of maybes. I've never seen you so wishy-washy."

"It's this Klein case. Scratch the surface of all the dislike that's surfacing, you fall into a pus pool of hatred."

"Reminds me of my cousins."

"Is this about the dead one?"

"They're not all dead. Anyway, these cousins were out west skiing. One stopped to see what was ahead, the other did a hockey stop above, knocked the first off his feet, which sent him over a jump he was eyeballing. He did a yard sale—ski clothes and gear spread across the slope, got two broken femurs, and fractured a c-spine. The rest of my cousins and me swear he also left some brains in the snow."

"Do any of your cousins have names?"

"Yeah, but I'm protecting the stupid."

"What does that story have to do with the case I'm discussing?"

"Don't know . . . jealousy?"

THIRTY-NINE

EDIE WALKED AROUND the Capitol, twice, then stood on the northwest corner of the square and looked down State Street. Now or never, she told herself. If anything happens today, I'm ready to take it on. The walk signal came on. Edie followed the hordes of people crossing North Carroll Street, and then followed a splinter group down State Street. Less than two blocks down State Street she stopped. She recognized the backs of two people as they stepped from a doorway that few people noticed as they scurried up and down the street. She stood and watched as the two people embraced, kissed, then parted. They need to get a room, she thought, but considering that it was her friend Uselman and Ashley Zielinski, maybe they were just coming from there. Zielinski headed one way, and Uselman walked toward Edie.

"You don't waste any time," Edie said when Uselman was a few feet from her.

He looked up, smiled, "Ain't getting any younger. Look who's being brave."

"It's either facing this street or find something to pulverize."

"Why the anger?"

"Family matters."

"They will get you every time. Where you headed?"

"One of the lunch carts on the library mall. I'm on a mission to save my sanity."

"May I join you?"

"Sure. Didn't you already have lunch?"

"An appetizer. I'll just keep you company."

They sat on the steps of St. Paul's while Edie drank a fruit smoothie, the only thing she thought she could keep down.

"How's it going today?" asked Mark.

"Besides being pissed at the world, nothing. You?"

"Lots of interesting pillow talk from Ashley. Mainly about politics. She seems to know a lot of people, and really likes to throw their names around."

"You impressed with that?"

"No, I can throw names around too. Doesn't mean much. Some of the people I know duck and run for cover when they see me. But I am intrigued with the names she is throwing; many are part of the ruling elite of the state. She certainly associates with a different level of people than me."

"But are they any better? Give me some those tidbits. I'd like to be in the know, early."

"Not till I get a handle on the story. A quick and dirty take on it is that it's more of the same shit, political cronyism disguised as being receptive to business. It's interesting enough that I'm going to dig deeper. How's the family?"

"Rocky."

"How come?"

"Found out Phil's been tracking me."

"So? Was it malicious?"

"He did it without my knowledge or consent."

"That's not good. You going to sue him, or move out on him?"

"Still trying to figure that out."

"Take your time. You two have been together a long time. Is this one blunder worth throwing everything away?"

"When did you become a therapist?"

"Went through the school of hard knocks. You know, something's been bugging me since our lunch. How did that guy from the pub—"

"Jake Thomas."

"How did Jake Thomas know you were back on duty?"

"Haven't given it any thought," said Edie, drifting into her own thoughts. "Maybe I was wrong about who Beelzebub is."

"What?"

"Beelzebub, that's who I thought LeRoy Theis was."

"A father of one of those kids?"

"And married to Madonna Theis."

"Oh. I have no idea what you're talking about."

"During my investigation last fall, the first time I met LeRoy Theis, the name Beelzebub popped into my brain."

"So?"

"I'm rethinking things. Back at the pub, what did you say about politics and money?"

"I don't remember."

"Something like politics and money are always bedfellows."

"That's nothing new, I say that all the time."

"LeRoy Theis and Jake Thomas. Jake Thomas and the Theises. Hmmm. I think I've got the wrong Beelzebub."

"What's got you interested? Come on, Edie, let me in on the ground floor."

"When this case is done, and the one after that, I think Mr. Thomas deserves a closer look. That sounds familiar, I think I've said that before. Whatever, this time I've got to follow up. Curious, isn't it, that Jake Thomas knew you? I've never seen your picture in the paper."

"I'm a reporter, lots of people know me. If he's got any political connections, they could have pointed me out to him."

"Still, it's curious."

When Edie returned from lunch there was a bouquet of balloons on her desk. On each, a man's face was drawn. The note read: "Sorry. Love, Phil." Edie flicked two of the balloons with her fingers, and then settled in to review her notes on the Klein case.

FORTY

EDIE WAS BACK in the office waiting for Erica Jones, Nicholas Klein's sister, to show up for an interview. She was late. *Why is everybody else's time more precious than mine?* She went to see Steve in the gangs unit.

Steve was finishing a report. "Be with you in a sec, Edie." He pushed enter, then looked up. "What can I do for you?"

"While I'm waiting for someone, thought I'd check up on Phil's problem. Know of any start-up gangs in that area?"

"No. I think that Phil's building was either a spring prank or malicious."

"Anything new with gangs?"

"Sorry, Edie, I'll catch you up on gangs later, but I've got to run. See you."

Edie heard a chuckle, turned around, and saw Gracie leaning in her office doorway.

"What's the matter, Detective, run him out of the office, too?" said Gracie.

"No ma'am, just asking about gangs."

"What are you doing in the office? Don't you have work to do?"

"Waiting for my next interview, she's late."

"How's the case going?"

"Getting silence and slime. Wondering what the next person will bring."

"You're about to find out. I think that's her," said Gracie, pointing at the office door.

Edie turned to see a five-foot-seven woman, blonde, with a distinct baby bump. Edie grabbed a tablet and pen and walked over to the woman. "Hi, I'm detective Edie Swift, and you are?"

"Erica Jones, Nick Klein's sister."

"Thanks for coming in, we'll go back to an interview room so we can talk in private."

Erica pulled the chair away from the table to accommodate her belly. "It feels good to sit down, been busy at the store. Could I have a chair to put my feet up on?"

Edie slid her chair over to Erica, who placed her feet on it. Edie brought a chair from the next room for herself.

"Again, thanks for coming in. For my records, would you tell me your name, age, and where you live?"

"Erica Jones, twenty-five, and I live as far away from Troutbeck as possible. Heard you moved in last fall, my condolences."

"What do you find wrong with Troutbeck?"

"Haven't been there long enough, have you? In my lifetime, there's been two murders, strip clubs, gossip all day long. I sacrificed my virginity to get out of there."

"That's drastic."

"It's all I could think of. I was five months pregnant when I graduated from high school. Got married the next day. The old busybodies keep telling me that they hadn't seen that since the 1950s. Who cares?"

"Ms. Jones, I was hoping you could tell my about your brother."

"When I was young, I always thought that he was a sweet kid, except when he was hanging with Jay. Boy, was I wrong."

"Why do you say that?"

"I've been getting an earful about his affairs. Poor Mariah, I should have warned her about my family."

"Did you know of anyone who wanted to harm your brother?"

"No, if it was Mariah that was dead, I'd say my brother Jay—he hated her."

"Why?"

"She took his sidekick away."

"Anything else you can tell me about your brother?"

"No. Hope you catch whoever did it."

"What can you tell me about your sister-in-law?"

"She came from La Crosse, fell in love with my brother. Always been good to me."

"Where were you the night of your brother's death?"

"Tossing and turning in my own bed, trying to get comfortable. Do you ask that of everyone?"

"Yes. Thank you for coming in. If you can think of anything else, my number is on the card." Edie handed her a business card and escorted her to the elevator. Well, there was no new slime, and a lot less of it than I expected, she thought, but nothing new to help me.

FORTY-ONE

PHIL OPENED THE garage door to find Edie holding her balloons in one hand, and pizza from their new favorite pizza joint in Sun Prairie. He took the pizza from her. "Did you get their salad and garlic bread?"

"Of course, they're still in the car."

"I'll put this in the kitchen, and then get the rest of the stuff out of the car. What are we going to feed Hillary?"

"I'll thaw some squash for her," Edie said following Phil in, then placing the balloons on the table where candles usually sat.

Edie and Phil sat down to dinner with Hillary strategically placed between them. Edie broke the silence. "I like your peace offering."

"I like your peace offering, too."

"Food does have a way of smoothing things over."

"Can't be angry on a full stomach," Phil agreed. They ate in silence that was punctuated by Hillary's babbling. "What's our next move?"

"Treat each other as adults," said Edie.

"At what age do you become an adult?"

"Don't know. I was going to say when you have children, but some of the calls I take would show that to be a lie. Maybe it's a process of becoming, and not so much that one day you're a kid, then the next day you're an adult."

"I don't know if I've reached it. Every day I wish my father was here to tell me what to do. Some of those days are worse than others."

"I would like to have met him, but he isn't here, so we have to muddle through the best we can."

"Watching my father, it looked easy. Thought I'd be the provider and protector—"

"And we would live happily ever after. Nice fairy tale, but those stories never went beyond that moment. They never got to where they were either muddling through life or punting. The boys always seemed to be doing something, even stupid stuff. The girls just seemed to be waiting. When I was young, I wanted to be the one doing stuff, not waiting for someone. I wanted to be the provider and protector."

"We can't both be—"

"Why not?"

"It never worked that way in my family."

"This isn't your family—it is ours. This is a new world. We decide what happens here."

"My mother's not going to like this."

"She doesn't have a say in it."

"She's not going to like that either."

"Tough."

The silence that followed was way beyond awkward. Edie knew her emotions were at fever pitch, and Phil looked as if he would explode if touched. But something had shifted in their relationship. Edie needed time to figure out what it was, and what the new direction they were heading toward was. For a moment she missed the early days of their relationship when such explosive emotions were ignited and they ended in a tangle of arms and legs, sweaty skin, and release. This time she needed to find another way down from this dizzying emotional height; she guessed Phil did too.

Later, as Edie sat at the kitchen table thumbing through the yearbooks that Bridget Briggs had left in her care, it was the older books that interested her most. The kids in these yearbooks were the contemporaries of her Aunt Jill and that other woman, her so-called mother, who abandoned her as an infant. But she had never found a yearbook from those times. Edie was excited to see what her parents' generation looked like when young. She was surprised to see that those kids looked washed—people were always calling them dirty hippies—that the girls had long straight hair, conservative clothes. The boys sported conservative haircuts. Collectively, they looked like a bunch of nice midwestern kids. There were the standard pictures of football games, basketball games, cheerleaders, plays, clubs, and dancing. It was hard for Edie to believe that these clean-cut kids would soon join their brothers and sisters to confront their country, demanding that it live up to its stated ideals. But, for a moment, those kids were suspended for all eternity in youth, at the time of their lives when they could dream that they had the power to set the world right. "Hey, Phil, can you come here for a moment?"

"Can it wait? I'm watching a game."

Edie walked out to the living room with the yearbook in hand, "Who does this look like?" she asked, holding the book in front of his face.

Phil took a glance at the picture Edie pointed to, "My mother." He handed the book back to Edie and went back to watching TV.

"And who else?"

"Edie, can't this wait?"

"Not for me. Besides, you are watching a baseball game. They'll give detailed replays if it's a good play. Now who is this other person?" Edie asked, placing the book in front of him again.

Phil pushed the book aside. "It's not the same. I want to see the play as it happens."

"See, a commercial's on, do you think they stop the game for a commercial? Take a look, please."

Phil took the book from Edie, "That's my mother. I've seen high school pictures of her before. Is that Mrs. Voss? Do you know what her maiden name was?"

"No, I don't know what her family name was. But those two look kind of cozy. Did you ever see Mrs. Voss and your mother talk this winter?"

"I introduced them once. I think they said hi. After that I was busy and thought two old ladies could take it from there."

Phil paged through the book until one photo caught his eye.

"What you looking at?" asked Edie.

"My father dancing at homecoming with Mrs. Voss. They look really cozy."

"Let me see," Edie took the book back. "Interesting."

"Can I have it back?"

"Later, your game is on." Edie went back to the kitchen to take a closer look. She turned back to the first page. This was interesting, she thought, seeing the older generation in their youth. What pictures will Hillary see of me? she wondered. She made a mental note to expunge any incriminating phots from Aunt Jill's stash of pictures. And maybe burn her yearbooks.

Before going to bed, Edie called Crystal Mitchell at work to set up a meeting. Crystal wanted the meeting early in the day, and someplace where the two of them wouldn't be seen by anyone. Crystal agreed to meet Edie at Phil's shop after work, on her way home, before the commuters joined the rush to Madison. Why didn't Crystal leave that message on Edie's phone? It would have been simple and easy thing to do, Edie thought after she hung up. Maybe Crystal was just paranoid.

On the way to bed, Edie passed Phil. He was still engrossed in the yearbook. She softly ran her hand across his shoulder blades, and he looked up and smiled. A moment later he clicked off the TV, then followed Edie. Delayed gratification could be a good thing.

FORTY-TWO

THE SUNRISE WAS glorious, a beautiful time of day; Edie wondered why she didn't visit it more often these days. Then she remembered she liked sleeping. Edie took another sip of coffee, looked at her watch, walked back into Phil's shop, and waited. The sunrise was nice to watch, but didn't anyone care that she hated waiting! Today, that anyone was Crystal Mitchell, and she was late.

This was the day and the time that Crystal insisted on. This was the place Edie suggested: Phil's shop where both cars would be under cover—away from prying eyes. Hearing a car, Edie opened an overhead door. Moments later, Crystal drove in. Edie closed the bay door, then walked over to the car and knocked on the window. "Are you getting out?"

"Anybody here?"

"Just you and me," Edie assured Crystal.

"Are you sure?"

"Yes, I checked the whole building. Inside and out."

Crystal got out of the car. "Where's the bathroom?"

"Back left corner."

Finished with the bathroom, Crystal stood in its doorway. "Any place without windows that we can talk?"

Edie walked into the equipment room. It was better not to argue with paranoid people, maybe they had a reason for their paranoia. Crystal followed her. Since this meeting was arranged for and by Crystal, Edie let her find the opening words.

When she began, Crystal spoke to the floor. "Mamie Robin was my best friend all the way through school. Met her in kindergarten and we walked through our high school graduation ceremony together. I was thrilled when she asked me to be her maid of honor. It was the start of our dreams. We used to plan that we'd live close to each other. I knew Tom would never take her away from here. That we would grow old together." Crystal wiped away her tears. "We had names picked out for our girls: Dakota Mamie for my first girl, Faith Crystal for hers. It was fun planning the wedding. I miss her. I lost the necklace she gave me, I want something of her back." Crystal took a deep breath. "Mr. Acker said he gave you the daisy necklace. Could I have it?"

"No."

"Please. I can't find mine. I feel like I've lost Mamie Robin all over again."

"No."

Crystal stood up, took a step toward Edie. Edie didn't move. Crystal took two steps back.

"Don't worry about the necklace, it's safe at the station," said Edie. Safe and sound at the sheriff's office with the other one, she thought to herself. "Is this all you wanted to talk about?"

Crystal resumed staring at the floor, "That night . . ." Crystal started then stopped talking.

"Which night was that?"

"The night Mamie Robin was . . ." Crystal stopped, smeared the tears across her face with her hands. "The night of Mamie Robin's death." There was a long silence. "That night she and I went to the mall, she was looking at baby clothes."

"Was Mamie Robin pregnant?"

"No. Hoping. She and Tom were trying. I thought that was funny. What newly married couple doesn't try?" Crystal's head jerked up. "What was that?" Crystal moved to a corner of the equipment room.

"A car passing by."

"It didn't turn in here, did it? It sounded like it did. Could you check?" asked Crystal, moving deeper into the equipment room.

Edie went to the door, no car was in the lot. She walked back to the equipment room and stood in the doorway. "There's no car outside."

Crystal didn't move from the dark corner she had retreated to. "Anyway . . . anyway that night I dropped Mamie Robin at her place, watched her walk through her door, it was the last I saw of her."

"Did you tell that to the police? Do you remember seeing anything out of place that night?'

"I don't remember what I said to the cops. No, nothing looked out of place. It was weird that night. I sat and watched her walk into her house, she turned on her light, and then waved to me, and it was as if I couldn't move from there."

"What happened next?"

"I went . . ."

A passing car backfired. Crystal flung herself on the cement floor. Edie gripped the handle of her ceramic coffee mug until it broke. She caught the cup before it hit the floor, lukewarm coffee splashed across her hand. Edie wiped the splashed coffee off on her jeans; she wondered if Crystal noticed what happened. Edie looked back at Crystal. The color had drained from Crystal's face, her eyes had grown big, her breathing was fast, and she looked like a scared animal searching for an exit, thought Edie.

"What was that?" Crystal whispered.

"A car backfiring."

"Damned if it was. Sounded like gunfire to me. I'm getting out of this death trap." Crystal ran for her car and started it.

Edie sprinted to open the bay door. Phil would never forgive her if the new bay door paint was ruined. When the door was up, Crystal blasted backward out of the shop, swung the car around as if she were an experienced demolition derby driver, then tore out of the lot.

Edie surveyed the scene. No cars were in sight, not even the usual commuters to Madison, just the sun rising in the sky. She closed the bay door, picked up her broken coffee mug, turned off the equipment room light, then walked out into the sunlight, whistling.

FORTY-THREE

EDIE ROCKED IN her office chair, with her right foot on the lower drawer of her desk controlling the speed, as she thought about Mamie Robin Brown's case. It had taken a few days to get the file from long-term storage. The pictures of Mamie Robin matched the description Troutbeck people had been telling Edie: Mamie Robin was sweet, maybe that was the memory Troutbeck wanted to avoid—the horrid death of one who barely began to live.

The pictures of the crime scene were horrific. A woman barely out of girlhood stabbed twenty-six times. Bleeding, raped, the young woman still fought back; the autopsy report noted hits to the face, wounds to her hands and arms that were consistent with defending herself. Semen that had been collected was never tested. Why the wait, wondered Edie. Was there an assumption that it was her husband's? No suspect had emerged? No money available? No time when there were more pressing cases? The thought that a woman wasn't important to a democracy popped into her brain. She tried to dismiss it, but it did hang around the edges of her thoughts. Edie had a growing admiration for that young woman. All the sweetness that everyone surrounding her had commented on covered a toughness that surfaced as she fought for her life.

Edie looked over the detective's report. Again, no forced entry seen: did Mamie Robin never lock her doors like the rest of Troutbeck, or did she know her killer? Everyone close to the deceased had accounted for their whereabouts at the time of her death, and Tom Brown's alibi had been the tightest. Like all the other nights at work, Tom was surrounded by his fellow employees, while working, on break, eating—Edie wondered if those guys also took a piss together. No one else was suspected. No new leads had come in over the years; the universe wasn't coughing up any new suspects. Silence reigned, again. Always silence. Why? What were people afraid of? Edie shook her head, was anyone ever going to talk? She returned the Mamie Robin file to storage. The only move Edie had left was to mine the memory of the investigating detective.

Gracie was in when Edie stopped back. "Come in, but don't talk to me until I'm finished with this paragraph." A moment later she looked up. "It's you, have a seat. What can I do for you?"

"What do you remember of the Mamie Robin Brown case?"

"Name's familiar. Why should I remember it?"

"I mentioned it a few days ago, and you were the lead detective on the case."

"Give me a few details."

"Young girl stabbed to death and raped, happened in Troutbeck."

Gracie dropped her head forward and seemed to be lost in thought. "Got it. My last case as a detective before I moved up."

"Off the record, what was your impression?"

Gracie stared for a moment at Edie. "Some new lead in that case?"

"No, but her name keeps popping up in the Klein case."

"Bloody. It was bloody. I thought the killer was someone the victim knew, couldn't prove it—everyone was accounted for."

"Was she raped before or after the stabbings?"

"Never knew, but the autopsy suggested she put up one hell of a fight. My guess was that she was raped as she was dying—a double asshole in my book." Gracie paused for a moment. "With that amount of blood, someone knew something and still doesn't have the guts to come forward."

"I'm running into a wall of silence in my case, too."

"Why are you digging deeper into the Brown case? You think the Brown and Klein cases might be connected?'

"Don't know."

"Then why are you in my office asking about a case that was some twelve years ago?"

"As I said, because every time I ask about Nicholas Klein, someone mentions her name. My gut reaction is that it's more than proximity."

"Are the people of Troutbeck associating one case with the other?"

"Maybe. There is one other person who keeps popping up in both cases, a Crystal Mitchell."

"Who is she?"

"Mamie Robin Brown's best friend for life, and, today, the closest thing Mariah Collins has to a friend in Troutbeck."

It took Gracie a few minutes to reply. "Wallflower, seemed scared of her own shadow. You thinking that she's the link between the two?'

"Maybe."

"Damn it, Edie, I'm not a mind reader, what are you thinking?"

"That I want to do a little setup. Bring Crystal Mitchell in here for a talk. I'd like you to be in plain sight when I do."

"A visual kick in the butt?"

"More like a reminder of her friend."

"You want me to be chewing someone's ass during this scenario?"

"No, calmly talking to someone, nod your head at me, or somehow acknowledge me when we pass by. I want a face-to-face view. Crystal works the graveyard shift; you may have to come in early."

"You buying the coffee?"

"If you're making the donuts."

Their conversation was interrupted by a clerk. "Excuse me, Edie, a woman says she has an appointment with you."

"Must be Holly Sundby," said Edie.

"Don't remember the name, but there's a lot of deputies willing to talk with her, if you're busy," replied the clerk.

"Seems like you better get out there before they make fools of themselves," Gracie said.

Edie escorted Holly to an interview room, just the two of them. She looked at Holly settle into the chair. This petite woman was, by all accounts, deadly.

"Thanks for coming in, Miss Sundby. Want to just clear up a few questions that were left open last time. You said you were at a pizza parlor on the night of Nicholas Klein's death. Could you be more specific?" Edie said.

"We've been talking about you. Just come out and say what you want to know. I was screwing Chad. Gotta problem with that?"

"Can he corroborate that?"

"Yeah."

"Can anyone else corroborate it?"

"I'm not into threesomes."

"You two were awake all night."

"With time off for sleep."

Edie wasn't going to move Holly from her alibi for that night; it was time to try a different angle. "Where do you keep your guns?"

"Locked up."

"May we take a look at them?"

"What for?"

"Checking all avenues to solve this crime."

"Why would I kill Nick after all these years?"

"You tell me."

"I didn't do it."

"Then let us check the guns."

"Over my dead body."

FORTY-FOUR

TO HELL WITH spring, Edie thought as she leaned against Crystal Mitchell's car in the dawn's first light. It's never coming, I'm tired of being cold, I want summer. The nursing home's day crew had trickled into the building one by one. The third shift crew seemed to be rushing out in bunches. Crystal's head was down when she came out. In the time Edie had known her, not once had that woman looked straight ahead. Her head was always bowed. Crystal broke off from the group and she walked to her car alone. It wasn't until she was next to her car that Crystal lifted her head. Too late. Edie was leaning against her car and was monitoring Crystal's approach. Crystal looked back at the ground, and then lifted her head, now with a smile on her face.

"Morning, Edie, nice to see you."

"Pleasure is all mine, Crystal. How are you doing this fine April morning? See you've recovered from our last talk."

"I'm fine. I was probably jittery because Lee's been gone a lot."

"Is he home now?"

"Yes," said Crystal, looking at her watch. "He'll be expecting me soon. He likes to start his day with a hot meal."

Edie knew that was a lie. She'd sent another deputy to check out Lee's work. He wasn't there. They hadn't seen him in a few days—on vacation, they assumed. And he wasn't at home. Edie drove past the house on the way to Madison. "Maybe he could pour himself a bowl of cold cereal today."

"He won't like that."

"Won't do him any harm. Might do him good. It was thought to be health food a long time ago. Besides, if he can get his own breakfast, it'll give you and me some time to talk."

"What more do we have to talk about?"

"Lots. Let's take this to a warmer, more private place, okay?"

"I can talk here."

"I was thinking my office might be better." Crystal had skipped one interview, run out on the second. Crystal knew something, and Edie wanted to find out what it was by any means within the letter of the law. She was not going to let Crystal go this time. Edie watched as blood drained from Crystal's face. "It's away from prying eyes and big ears."

"Do I need a lawyer?'

"I don't know, do you?"

"Am I being charged with anything?'

"No, we're just going to talk, see if you can clear up a few things about Nick Klein for me."

"Okay, I'll follow you."

"I'd rather you rode with me."

"What am I going to tell Lee?"

"That you talked with me. The truth is always easier to remember. If not the truth, you can say there was a traffic accident on the eastbound beltline or someone from the day shift came in late and you were asked to stay over. You know your husband better than me, you'll know what he will believe."

Crystal sat in the front seat with Edie, working the window buttons. "Do you want me to turn my phone off?"

"Why would you do that?" Edie turned on the window control.

Crystal put her hands on her lap and stared at them. "He might be tracking me?"

"Who is this he?"

"Lee."

"If you want to, you can turn off your phone. You know what's best. If your husband is tracking you, what are you going to tell him about the phone being off?

"I stayed late to help out. Management doesn't like us to carry our personal phones during work. And I turned it off to save the battery," said Crystal as she turned off her phone, then hugged the passenger's door.

To Edie, it sounded like a well-practiced excuse.

Gracie Davis had arranged the scene as Edie requested: she and a deputy were in the hallway talking when Edie and Crystal stepped off the elevator. She stopped talking and watched as Edie and Crystal walked past. Gracie nodded at Edie, then resumed talking after Edie and Crystal passed by.

Edie noted a flicker of recognition cross Crystal's face as they passed by Gracie. She guided Crystal to an interview room, cozy, windowless, two chairs, a small table pushed up against the wall with a recording device on it.

"This is it?" asked Crystal.

"Not much to look at, but it's functional. Can I get you something to drink?"

"Coffee, please."

"Black?"

"With sugar."

"I'll be back in a few moments. Please, make yourself comfortable." Edie closed the door to the interview room behind her, and then flipped the sign to "in use." Five minutes alone should do it, thought Edie.

Five minutes later, Edie was back with coffee and donuts for both of them. She handed Crystal a cup and some sugar packets, placed the donuts on the table within reach of both of them.

"Thought cops went out for donuts," said Crystal.

"Only when we are on the road and it's our break time. Hope you enjoy the donuts, they were a special order. Crystal, I'm going to record our conversation," Edie said as she turned on the recorder.

"Why?"

"Keep us both honest."

While Edie stated date, time, and the participants, Crystal emptied the sugar packets into her coffee, stirred it, and took two bites of a donut. Edie waited for Crystal to state her name, then remained silent waiting for Crystal to begin.

"Why am I here?" said Crystal, her fingers weaving through each other.

"To talk about Nicholas Klein. To continue our talk of a few days ago—uninterrupted."

"Who's the black woman that we passed in the hallway when we came in?"

"Lieutenant Davis. Do you know her?"

"I think I've seen her before, a long time ago. Has she been here long?'

"I know that she's been here more than twelve years. Never really asked her how long she's been on the force."

"She might have been the one who talked to me when Mamie Robin died." Crystal looked down at her hands, clasped for a moment in her lap, then her fingers began to work themselves into knot, then untwisted those knots to begin again with a new pattern; it looked as if they searching for a way out of a maze. "I'm a good girl," she whispered.

Edie waited. Crystal kept her head down, her hair veiled her face.

"Who says you're not?" asked Edie.

"My husband. And my mother."

"Why?"

"He thinks I'm having an affair. My mother was always telling us about the girls who slept with their boyfriends before they got married. Sluts every one of them, she'd say," Crystal said to her hands, as they turned her wedding ring up and down and around on her ring finger.

Edie remained silent, wondering how fast she should push the conversation.

Crystal made the leap. "He always thinks I'm up to no good. Like when we got married. We were doing *it* before we got married. I didn't get my period that month, I thought I was pregnant. I told Lee that I was pregnant. I couldn't tell my mother anything. She would have called me a slut, like she did those other girls. And my best friend was dead, I didn't have anyone. So I told Lee. We eloped. A week after we got married, I got my period. He said I tricked him into marrying me. He's been calling me a slut ever since."

"That's not right."

"Does your husband ever say that to you?" Crystal asked.

Apparently not everyone in Troutbeck had gotten the message about her marital status. And Crystal didn't need to know it now. "No. The first time he does will also be the last time."

Crystal raised her head, a defiant look on her face. Her hands lay quiet in her lap. "This time I proved him right. I was having an . . . an affair with someone."

Edie wondered how deep the floodwaters of Crystal's emotions were that they spilled out now.

"He was so sweet. Sent flowers to me at work, Nick . . ." Crystal's hand flew to her mouth as if she could stuff her words back in. She resumed her position—staring at her hands, which again lay tightly clasped in her lap.

For Edie, it was time to push the envelope. "Nick who?"

It was moments before anyone spoke.

"Nick Klein," Crystal said.

"Tell me about it."

"He was a sweet man. He knew what Lee was like. It just happened. Lee was off on one of his hunting trips, Mariah had gone to help her mom, and Nick and me ran into each other at the Rooster's Crow and started to talk." Crystal looked at Edie. "If he was my man, I'd never leave his side."

"Why?"

"Nick always was a hound dog, even in high school, always sniffing after some girl, but he was sweet to each of them."

"What do you mean each of them?"

"Nick always told Lee about the other women. Lee thought it was funny that Mariah was getting screwed over."

"Crystal, where were you the night Nicholas Klein was killed?"

"In the cemetery with him."

"Why?"

"Nick wanted to talk."

"In the cemetery?"

"We often met there. It's a short walk from both our houses, away from the road. No busybodies to see us. No one to hear us. It's not a place anybody has an interest in at night. It was just us two."

"What happened that night?"

"Nick broke up with me. Said Mariah wanted a divorce. Said that he realized that he loved Mariah, and hoped it wasn't too late for them. He knew he wanted her back. He was going to do whatever it took to get her back. He was going to show her that he could live up to his marriage vows."

"What happened next?"

"I walked over to Mamie Robin's grave, then I heard a gunshot, looked back at Nick, saw him slump over. I ran."

"Why did you run?"

"I was scared. Scared that Lee had found out about me and Nick. He always said that he'd kill me if I ever left him. Seems like Lee couldn't stand to be with me, and didn't like the idea of me being with someone else."

"Had Lee found out about you and Nick?"

"I don't know. When I ran home, he wasn't there. I checked his gun locker, one was missing."

"Crystal, do you think your husband, Lee Mitchell, shot Nicholas Klein?"

"Lee's scary," Crystal said, twisting her fingers.

Too close to the bone, thought Edie. She needed to back off, give Crystal time to absorb the possibility. "Was that your daisy chain necklace I found near Mamie Robin's grave?"

Crystal continued talking to her hands. "Yes. Could I have it back?"

"No. It is part of an ongoing investigation."

"But I didn't kill Nick or Mamie Robin!"

Edie took the opening. "Who do you think killed your friend Mamie Robin Brown?"

"I don't know," Crystal whispered to her hands.

"Where were you the night of Mamie Robin Brown's death?"

"At my place, waiting for Lee. He was late."

"Did he show up?"

"Yes, he was late and bloody."

"Did he give you an explanation for the blood?"

"Lee said there had been an accident at work and that he had helped stop the bleeding and bandage the guy up. Said he was sorry that he hadn't changed. Said he didn't want to be extra late coming to my place."

"Did you believe him?"

"Yes, I believe everything he tells me—I'm scared of him."

"What did you find special about Lee Mitchell?"

"He was the only boy in school to look at me. It was as if the others didn't see me. And that's okay because Lee and me have the wildest sex, especially after he's been hunting. Bet those high school boys would be jealous, if they knew."

"Crystal, did you and Lee have sex the night Mamie Robin was killed?"

"The best sex . . ." Crystal didn't finish the sentence. She went white, her hands started to shake, sobs wracked her body. To Edie, Crystal seemed to shrink into herself and almost disappear.

"Crystal, at this time, I think I need to ask if you would like a lawyer."

"I don't know any."

Edie let Crystal's sobs subside before she continued, "Crystal, is your husband at home?"

"No."

"Do you know where your husband is?"

"He never tells me where he's going."

"Do you know where he likes to go?"

"His hunting shack."

"Where is that?"

"He never took me, says women don't belong at his shack."

"Where is his hunting shack?"

"Overheard him tell some of his buddies it's somewhere north of a town called Partyville."

"Partyville?"

"I think he's making it up, I can't find it on a map."

A deputy sat with Crystal while Edie talked with Gracie. "You wrote in your reports on the Mamie Robin Brown case that Crystal said Lee Mitchell was with her all night."

"If I wrote it, then that is what she said. Is she saying something different now?"

"Yes, I think we have a good suspect in the Brown case, and probably the Klein case—Lee Mitchell."

"Did Crystal say that?"

"I taped our conversation. She didn't state that her husband murdered anyone, but she put him in first place as a suspect."

"What about spousal privilege?"

"She might waive that, if she knows that Lee might spend the rest of his life in jail. I'd like to keep her here."

"Have you charged her with anything?"

"Not yet."

"We can hold her as a material witness for now, and work with the DA about other possible charges. What's your next move?

"Finding Lee Mitchell, he's got a hunting shack north of Partyville."

"That would be Pardeeville with a d. It's in Columbia County. Check his home and work before going on a wild-goose chase."

"Deputies are already doing that," said Edie.

"I'll get the ball rolling for a warrant for Mitchell, and inform the Columbia County sheriff of our plans," said Gracie.

Edie turned to leave.

"Edie, remember, if you go, you are the backup; it is not your county."

FORTY-FIVE

PHIL GOT THE first call from Edie—she might be late, she had an errand to run in the next county. Aunt Jill got the second call: please, please take Hillary home to Troutbeck. With her life arranged, Edie headed north out of Madison on Highway 51. She became hyperalert near DeForest—the traffic flow pattern was new, but how many local drivers, she wondered, shifted to automatic pilot once outside of Madison. Where the highway narrowed down to two lanes Edie noted that people became sensible drivers, a benefit of driving a marked squad, or maybe they learned to read the road signs.

Edie met Columbia County Deputy Art Hill at the gas station at the corner of Highways 51 and 60. She handed him the arrest warrant for Lee Mitchell and the coordinates for the piece of land owned by the suspect.

"Hmmm, that's in rolling hills and Amish country."

"What?"

"These coordinates put the shack in lots of rolling hills covered with woods. That land was once farmed, and the least productive land was then sold for hunting. That cut the size of good farmland down to where farming became a hobby. Most people can't afford to do it as hobby, so the Amish came in and they are making a living among those hills."

"What has that got to do with this case?"

"Well, it might be slow going if we get behind some Amish buggies. And when we get to this guy's land we may have to walk a bit. Got your walking shoes on? May even need boots due to the snowmelt." Deputy Hill looked at the warrant. "Looks in order. Follow me. We'll take a shortcut. Don't want to backtrack to Highway 22."

Edie groaned as she walked back to her squad. She was learning that in rural areas there were no such things as shortcuts.

She was right. She followed Deputy Hill across Highway 51 into the rolling hills of the Wisconsin River watershed in Columbia County. Edie didn't bother to keep track of the miles in the so-called shortcut, but when they turned right into more rolling hills she knew it was going to be a long drive. Maybe she should have sent the warrant to Columbia County and been done with it—let those deputies pull Mitchell out of his hunting shack. She couldn't back out now, might as well make the most of it and enjoy the scenery.

Driving through Wyocena and Pardeeville, Edie noticed heads turning. She imagined that she and Deputy Hill would be the gossip of the day at supper. How many Facebook inquiries would be generated as they drove through those towns? Tomorrow morning, how many people would ask if there was any news about Columbia and Dane County sheriffs being in their neighborhood? Edie hoped the unfolding story would be minor, a story fit to be buried near the ad section, if it even made the news.

Edie parked on the dirt field road behind Deputy Hill, radioed dispatch that she was out of the county and out of the vehicle, put on her bulletproof vest, then walked over to Hill's squad.

"What's this guy like?" Deputy Hill asked before he looked up and saw Edie in her vest.

"Haven't met him. General opinion is that he's an asshole."

"Is he a survivalist?" asked Hill as he put on his bulletproof vest.

"Don't know. We know he's an avid hunter. He's got the reputation of being a crack shot."

"Any ties to Posse Comitatus or claiming to be a sovereign person?"

"None that is known. Thought the Posse was defunct."

"Probably is, more likely it's being resurrected under a different name. Guess what I'm asking you is, do I need more than my handgun? And do we have enough manpower?"

"No idea. How far of a hike is it likely to be? Whatever we carry in, we have to carry out."

"But I'd rather have firepower handy instead of regretting I left it in the squad."

"I'm in your county. I'll follow your lead."

"I'll take my rifle. Your choice as to what extra firepower that you carry." Deputy Hill looked over the GPS on his cell. "Hope this isn't uphill both ways. Either way we'll be sweating bullets with these vests on. Ready?"

"Yup. Lead away, you got the scout position."

Edie followed Hill through land that was once farmed but now grew weeds that caught on her uniform pants, and hid decaying cornstalk stubble for her to stumble over. She was grateful to be wearing her uniform and boots, but with the beating those clothes were taking she wouldn't be able to postpone clothes shopping any longer.

At the edge of the woods was a truck. Deputy Hill checked it out while Edie, with pistol drawn, was his backup. The doors were locked and no one was hiding in the cab.

"Suspicious guy, only out-of-towners lock their vehicles around here," said Hill. "Nothing in the back, nothing visible on the floor. Racks for two guns, gotta assume he has both with him, if not more."

"First time I've liked assuming anything."

Hill looked around. "Don't see any signs of a shack nearby, we'll have to go deeper." He headed into the woods.

Edie stood still.

Five minutes later Hill returned. "Thought you were right behind me."

"Sorry, had to take a piss," said Edie, hoping that Hill would buy her excuse.

"Next time tell me. Keep that whistling up, I've heard that bears have been sighted in the area last week," said Hill, walking a few feet into the woods. He turned back. "Come on, we're burning daylight."

"Bears? Didn't know they had moved this far south."

"Don't you ever read the papers? They've been sighted around these parts and farther south for years. Best to keep your eyes open."

"I lived in the middle of Madison then, never figured it would concern me. Now, what type of bear signs am I supposed to be looking for?"

"Prints in the mud, scat, fur on trees that they used to scratch themselves. They are coming out of their winter dens and they're hungry after not eating all winter. Mostly keep your eyes open for mama bears and their cubs."

"If I see them, what should I do?"

"Don't come between them. If you do, then kiss your ass good-bye. Let's go get this guy."

Edie commanded her feet to move. This time they listened. Confronting criminals was one thing, but she knew nothing about bears. The only time she'd seen a bear was at the Vilas Zoo and it was behind bars and in a deep pit. She wasn't interested in seeing one today in the middle of nowhere. Though Deputy Hill made it sound as if she needed to read up on bears, if she continued to live in Troutbeck, which she knew was on the outskirts of civilization and now was near bear country.

Edie and Deputy Hill walked single file through the woods following the contours of the hills, and then followed the creek until it became marshy land. Hill raised his hand. "I appreciated your whistling—it kept the bears alert to our presence—but you gotta stop it now. I think we're at the hunting shack," he said as Edie came up alongside him. He pointed to the opening ahead of them. There on the far side of the creek, at the forest's edge, was a hunting shack. Rustic, no windows, a hunter's paradise, according to Deputy Hill's assessment. "See the smoke? Looks like someone is home." Hill led the way across the creek, motioned to Edie that she should establish a perimeter where the tall grasses ended. He went up to the door and knocked. "I'm looking for a Lee Mitchell?"

"Who are you?"

"Columbia County Deputy Art Hill, I've got a warrant for the arrest of a Lee Mitchell. Is that you?" Sounds of bolts being shoved into place were heard.

"Go to hell," yelled Lee, followed by the sound of more bolts being shoved into place.

Hill backed away from the shack, quickly. He re-joined Edie at the edge of the clearing. "Mr. Mitchell, we'd just like to talk."

"Not talking to nobody."

"Got a warrant for your arrest. Do you understand what that means?"

"Goody. This is what I think of that." There was a shotgun blast from inside the shack through the door.

"Now why did you go and ruin a good hunting shack?"

"It's mine. I can do what I want with it."

Hill and Edie moved farther away, found a secure place to squat down in line with the corner of the shack, yet out of sight of the hunting shack.

"Should I read him his Miranda rights?" Deputy Hill asked Edie. "I can't say that he's really in our custody right now."

"No, he's not in custody, but I've been told this is your county, so it's your call. We'll let the lawyers do the nitpicking later. This guy is my top suspect in a murder case, possibly involved in a prior murder. I don't want him to walk away on a technicality."

Deputy Hill yelled the Miranda warning to Mitchell. Lee answered with another blast from his shotgun.

"What do we do now?" asked Hill.

"Call for backup." Edie looked at her cell. "I'm not getting any coverage out here in these hills."

Hill looked at his cell. "Neither am I. Maybe I can get through to dispatch on my radio, then they can patch me through to the sheriff. Situations like this, he wants to be the first to know. I may have to climb a tree to get coverage."

"You try that. I'll see if I can get Mitchell to talk." Edie's thighs burned as she advanced in a low-profile squat toward the shack, stopping when she judged she was still at a safe distance from it. "Lee, this is Detective Edith Swift."

"There's two of you? When did they let sluts like you into the department?"

Edie regretted not bringing her rifle. "Mr. Mitchell, I've been trying to talk to you for the past few weeks."

"Been busy."

"I understand, but I'd still like to talk with you."

"'Bout what?"

"Your friend Nick Klein."

"He ain't no friend. Never was. Found that out too late."

"Everyone says he was."

"Friends don't screw your wife."

"She misses you."

"More like she misses that nobody's around to fuck her anymore."

"She's really upset that you're not at home."

"'Cause she doesn't know what I'll do to her next."

Hill crawled up to Edie. "Backup will be here in twenty, maybe thirty minutes. They're asking for mutual aid from Marquette. Keep him talking."

"Don't know what you mean, Lee," Edie yelled. Then she whispered to Hill, who was crawling away from her, "What are you going to do?"

"That bullet was meant for the slut," shouted Lee.

"What bullet?" Edie yelled back.

"The one that took down traitor Nick."

Hill stopped, turned to Edie, and whispered, "I've got a plan, just keep him talking."

"Don't do anything stupid. We'll have backup in twenty minutes," Edie whispered back.

"Don't worry, I know what I'm doing."

Edie watched as he got up and ran for the woods. She lost sight of him among the dense undergrowth of

241

the woods when he took a left turn toward the shack. She dropped her head and whispered to the ground, "Was I ever that stupid?" Edie's brain presented her with a slideshow of herself at age thirteen, getting on a bus heading for Florida with a letter of permission from Aunt Jill, which Edie had forged, and money she had stolen from Aunt Jill for the ticket and food on the way. It jumped forward to the time she went skinny-dipping in the high school principal's hot tub with her friends Tim and Al. Then fast-forwarded to her getting drunk at campus frat parties. Worse, the times she went alone to frat parties. Then there was her solo ice sailing, in a rig that she had borrowed from some unknown person, across Lake Mendota. "Shit, I thought a life review was supposed to come at the end of your life. This can't be the end. Please, don't let this be the end. Damn, I didn't think I was that stupid. It looks like I'm lucky to be alive in spite of my stupidity."

Edie lifted her head, scanned the woods for Hill, spotted him as he pulled his shoeless self onto the roof of the shack with a chunk of wood in his hand, "Damn, he's stupider than me. And now I've got to try to keep him alive. Please, please, whatever, whoever is out there, forgive me my stupidity," whispered Edie. "Hey, Lee, nice place you got here," yelled Edie, in an attempt to keep him talking and not listening to the movements on the roof.

"Yeah, a home away from all the morons."

"Peaceful out here."

"Yeah, nothing bothers me out here."

"What about the animals?"

"Shot the ones that came around, nothing moves now when I'm here."

"Is that why you wanted to hurt Crystal—she bothers you?"

"I didn't want to hurt Crystal, I wanted to kill her . . . still do."

Edie mentally ticked off lawyerly objections to what she was about to say, but she couldn't miss the opportunity. A statement was a statement. His Miranda rights had been read to him. It would be up to Lee Mitchell to respond. A second later she shouted back, "But you missed."

"I got that bastard Nick instead. Next time it'll be the whore I married that I get."

"You married her, don't you love her?" Edie watched as Hill plugged the chimney with his shirt and a chunk of wood, then sat on the roof's edge dangling his legs and looking at her before lowering himself to the ground, then running to the woods.

"Can't love a whore, they're only good for one thing."

"Why do you keep calling her that?"

"She lied to me. Said she was pregnant, she had to get married. All she wanted was for me to put a ring on her finger."

"Maybe she thought—"

"No, she was one more lying bitch."

Edie didn't respond. Hill was in the safety of the woods and making his way back to her.

"Know how to tell when a woman's lying? Their lips are moving," yelled Lee.

"Was Mamie Robin lying?" In the silence that followed, Edie wondered if she had pushed Mitchell too far.

"That bitch was doing that moron Tom Brown in high school. At least she got one good fuck before she died."

"Why do men think that a good fuck cures everything?" Edie whispered. She felt Hill flop on the ground beside her.

"Because it works for men. Did I hear him say that he shot anything that moved around here?" Hill whispered back.

"Yes."

"That's not right. We may be able to add some shooting out of season charges, the bastard. Who's this Mamie Robin?" he asked while he was lacing up his boots.

"Cold case. Young woman murdered about twelve years ago."

"You think he did it?"

"You just heard him admit to it," whispered Edie to Hill, then shouted to Mitchell, "Lee, how'd she die?"

"Squealing with joy," Lee shouted.

"That was quite some risk you took," whispered Edie to Hill.

"You kept him talking. That lessened the risk a bit."

"Where'd you come up with the idea of smoking him out?"

"An old family story that my grandmother told about her mother; it may be a story from a few more generations back than that."

Edie waited to learn more. "Well, aren't you going to tell me the whole story?"

"Sorry, was wondering how long it would take to smoke him out with those holes in the door. Anyway, this great-grandmother was a little itty-bitty thing who taught in a one-room schoolhouse. One day the older boys pushed her out of the school, and then locked the doors. She climbed up on the school roof. Put a board across the chimney, which smoked all the kids out. Thought it might work here."

"What happened then?"

"Don't know. But I think that when the story got around the community the boys who did the crime got their hides tanned by their fathers."

Edie and Hill turned their attention back to the shack. They could see wisps of smoke escaping from the cracks in the building.

"Damn, that looked better built. This may take a while."

It didn't. Lee Mitchell came out of the door blasting away with his shotgun. But coughing and blinded by the smoke.

Edie and Hill hugged the ground until the shooting was done.

Lee dropped to the ground rubbing his eyes. Smoke billowed from the shack.

Edie and Hill, with guns ready, sprinted to Lee as Edie shouted to drop his twelve-gauge shotgun.

"Get on the ground, face down," commanded Edie. "Lee Mitchell, you are under arrest for the murder of Nicholas Klein and Mamie Robin Brown." From her pocket she pulled a card with the Miranda warning printed on it. She wanted to get this right. No way was she going to be the reason Mitchell would walk away from two murder charges because of a technicality.

Lee kept rubbing his eyes until Hill handcuffed him.

Hill turned to look at the shack. "Got him?" he asked Edie.

"Yes," replied Edie.

"I better go unplug the chimney, don't want to burn down a perfectly good hunting shack."

FORTY-SIX

HAROLD ACKER SAT on the newly scrubbed bench where Nick Klein had died. The one he paid for so he could sit and talk to his Mamie. "Darling, they caught the bastard. It took time, but they got the SOB and I lived to see it. Thank God, I lived to see it. It was Lee Mitchell. I can't believe it was one of us. I'll never speak his name again. May he burn in Hell for all eternity. Brought these for you." He laid a bouget of lavender-colored garden phlox on her grave. "Miss you. See you soon." Harold pushed off the bench, picked up the daisies that he had laid on the bench next to him, then his cane, and then carefully made his way to Mamie Robin's grave and placed the daisies on her grave. "Little darling, I am so sorry. It's good to know you fought till the end, that you had something of me in you." Harold leaned on his cane and stretched as far as he could to get the kinks out of his back He looked around. It was a glorious spring day. "Well, darlings, I've got work to do. See you tomorrow."

The news spread rapidly through Troutbeck that Harold Acker was out walking the town. Most of the residents stopped their yardwork to watch his slow progress. A few asked if he needed a ride. He shook his head no as he continued his walk north to the edge of town.

At the last house in Troutbeck, he stopped, knocked, and waited for someone to answer.

Phil opened the door. "Mr. Acker."

"Is the missus home?"

Phil's smile spread to become a twinkle in his eyes. "Edie, it's Mr. Acker. He wants to talk to the missus. I guess that's you."

Edie came to the door carrying Hillary. She resisted jabbing Phil in the ribs. "Hi, Harold, come on in."

"No thanks, Edie, just stopped to say thank you."

"For what?"

"Getting the bastard."

"Only doing my job, sir."

"You done it well. Thanks." Harold took hold of Hillary's foot, shook it up and down until she giggled. "You got a cutie there."

"Takes after me," said Edie.

"I hope so. Take good care of her." Harold turned to walk back into Troutbeck.

"Harold, can we give you a lift home?" asked Edie.

"No, I'd like to enjoy this beautiful day."

Edie, Phil, and Hillary watched from their doorstep as Harold walked slowly back into the village.

"Well, missus, what are we going to do today?"

Edie shoved her elbow into Phil's gut.

"Ouch, police brutality."

"I'm not on duty."

About the Author

Julia C. Hoffman lives in Wisconsin with her husband. Her first book, Enemy Within, received an IPPY (Independent Publishers) Award in the Great Lakes Regional Division.

Books available at Amazon.com and other bookstores.

Also available on Kindle and other devices.

Author's Website: juliachoffman.com

Made in the USA
Middletown, DE
30 May 2016